Town Full of Secrets

Cheyenne Scrivens

Published by Cheyenne scrivens, 2022.

TOWN FULL OF SECRETS

First edition. June 22, 2022.

ISBN: 979-8227717696

Written by Cheyenne Scrivens.

Prologue

"So, you are going to where?" Taiki demanded.

"Goldenleaf," Ljerka answered. "Before you ask, I'm staying for two months."

"Two months?! Why two months?"

"Yes, two months. I have to do a lot of research to do."

"Answer the question, right?"

"Basically, yes."

Her friend Taiki left Ljerka to pack a few moments. She then returned with wine and snacks. She sat on her friend's bed as she drank her wine.

"So, tell me about Goldentree," Taiki requested.

"Goldenleaf. I don't know really but I am going to find out," Ljerka answered.

Ljerka finished packing. She then grabs her wineglass and takes a sip. She sat down on her bed next to her suitcase. She then slid the suitcase off the bed with Taiki's help and set it on the floor next to it.

"When do you leave?" Taiki asked.

"The day after tomorrow. First, I must contact someone about where to stay," Ljerka said. Seeing her face. "I know. I know. I should have contacted someone earlier, but I couldn't get through."

"Couldn't get through, why?" Taiki demanded. "Don't they have phones?'

"Probably. As I said I don't know much about Goldenleaf. Someone just sent me an email to go to..."

"Goldenleaf," finishing Ljerka's sentence then asked. "Who was it from?"

"I don't know. They didn't leave me a name."

"You are just going there without a plan and place to stay," she watched as Ljerka nodded. "That's really out of the box for you."

"Not really," then Taiki gave her a look. "Okay, maybe so but Goldenleaf has the answers."

"If you say so."

"I know so. Just watch."

Chapter 1

Ljerka has been in Goldenleaf for one week and she hasn't found any clues about her past. She became a regular little tourist. She visited every shop on foot. She went into one of the shops. They were hanging up decorations for the festival they were having. She saw cut outs of different sex positions. She blushes a little as she looks around.

"What can I do for you today, ma'am?" the store clerk asked.

"Just looking around," Ljerka answered. Curiosity got the best of her. "Why are you putting up..." she blushed again.

"Oh, the decorations... They are for the Sin Festival," he said. "It starts tonight at moonrise. You should stop by."

"I don't know..." Ljerka hesitated.

"If you want to come, it'll be at the Underfield Spring House." Then wrote down the address on a business card and gave it to her. "Wear something comfortable and also bring a robe."

"Why a robe..." then looked at the store clerk who raised an eyebrow. "Never mind and thank you."

Ljerka decide to leave and go back to her room to rest.

"Naheem, you didn't have to scare her," his sister scolded.

"Seija, I didn't do it on purpose," Naheem countered. "She seems curious."

"No, you want her," Seija countered.

"Of course, I do," he admitted. "She's hot. Also, she looks like..."

"No. No. No. No!"

"Yes," smiling.

"Damn it!" walking off.

Naheem continued smiling.

Meanwhile, Ljerka was in her room debating whether to go to the Sin Festival. It seemed interesting and she haven't had sex in a while. She looked up the history of the town and the Sin Festival. Both were interesting.

The founder of Goldenleaf and the Sin Festival was a couple named Elvire and Willamar Henriksen in 1506. They started the Sin Festival in 1546. The Festival of Sin was the third weekend of every month. It was Friday afternoon. Moonrise is at 3:30 pm. I have two hours to decide, she thought.

Later that night, Ljerka dreamed of making love to the store clerk that rang her out. It felt as if he was there with her. Touching her. Kissing her. Inside her.

"Mmm," Ljerka moaned out loud in her sleep.

She felt him pump into her fast and hard. "Aahh," she moans before she climaxed. "Shit!" she heard him moan.

Ljerka's eyes shot open as she sat up. She looked around in the dark. She got up and went in the bathroom in her room. She turned on the light. She looks herself in the mirror.

"Aahh," she screams.

She was butt ass naked. How did she become naked? Ljerka asked herself. Her skin felt tight. She ran her hands on her body as she thought about the dream.

"Damn," she moaned. "Mmm."

Ljerka stopped and left the bathroom. She grabbed her robe and flats then they put it on. She then grabbed her keys. She left the room then left the Inn. She walked towards the Underfield Spring House.

Ljerka was a block away when Naheem felt her coming down the street. She is the one, he thought. She's the one.

"She is coming," Naheem said to Jaxon.

"Good," Jaxon said. "Good."

"I'm going to meet her," Naheem said putting on his robe and left.

Naheem walked out the house and down the street to Ljerka. As he made it down, he thought of Eve. She looks just like her. After Eve's sudden death, he was somewhat heartbroken. When he saw the woman with Eve's face, he became instantly attracted to her.

Ljerka stopped a few feet from the man from the store.

"What am I doing?" she asked a loud. She began to turn around but the pull towards him and the house had her going forward.

She stopped in front of him.

"You came," was all he said before kissing her.

Pulling away, Ljerka pushed him away. He just kissed her neck. "Wait, I don't even know you." At least she thought she didn't.

"I am Naheem," he said pausing before taking her lips again.

She pulls away again. "Naheem, I'm Ljerka."

"Enough talking. Follow me," Naheem said taking her hand and leading to the house.

"No, I can't. I can't." stopped walking.

"Yes, you can. You came this far," pulling her a long.

Naheem walked towards the side door. He opened the door and pulled her inside. He then pulled her up two flights of stairs. He pulled her into the nearest room and closed the door then locked it. He began kissing her again. He then began untying and disrobed her. She started to pull back, but he kept her to him.

"No leaving, Ljerka, "Naheem said. "You came to me for a reason. I can help you with that."

"How could you possibly know?" Ljerka demanded. "How could…"

Naheem kissed her once again. More passionate this time. He disrobed himself. His robe landed next to hers on the floor. He kicked it to the side as he walked her to the bed.

Ljerka let herself be walked to the bed. She looks at Naheem's body. God, he was hot, she thought. His cock was...her thought drifted off when he licked her already hard nipples.

"Shit!" she moans as she reached to stroke his cock.

"Mmm," he moans as he felt her stroke him.

He reached between them to finger her clit and pussy. They pumped against each other hands. Before he could climax, Naheem stopped Ljerka's hand from stroking him. He felt climax with his fingers.

"Aahh...Fuckkk!" she moans but she felt him enter her.

Naheem fucked her like the dreams she been having, only better. It seems so natural, she thought. She wrapped her legs around Naheem's waist.

"Aahh," Ljerka moans again. She moves to him. "Aahh," she continues to moan.

Naheem pumps into Ljerka fast and hard. He leans down to take her moans in his mouth with his kiss. He then rolls onto his back. He moves his hips up to meet hers.

She sits back to break their kiss. She knelt on her knees and rode him. Ljerka felt his hands grip her waist.

"Open your eyes," Naheem ordered.

Ljerka opened her eyes. They were glowing. She continued to ride Naheem's cock. She moans again.

They climax together. Their climax rocked them. Ljerka arched her back like a bow. Naheem sits up in the sitting position to kiss on her neck. He ran his hands up and down her back then around to her breasts. He takes them into his mouth.

"Aahh," Ljerka moans.

Naheem took her up again. He felt her pussy tighten around his cock. "Shit!" he moans before kissing her. He climaxed and then he emptied himself into her.

They lay next to each other. Ljerka laid her head on his sweaty chest. Naheem wrapped one his arm around her.

"Wow, that was..." Ljerka started to say.

"Great. Amazing," Naheem said throwing out words.

"Either one," she said.

"I'll use astounding," he chuckles.

"Fine," she chuckles then climbed back on his cock. It was already hard. "Mmm," she moans as she slid down onto him.

Ljerka rode his cock, slow and sensual. She watched him while her eyes once again glowed. She watched how his eyes glowed, also. She wasn't scared but intrigued by it.

"She's going to be a problem," a woman commented.

"I know," another woman said.

"Her sister..."

"Is dead. If she's a problem, she will be too."

A man walked over to them. "What are you two doing here all a lone?" he asked them.

"Just looking," one of the women said.

The man grabbed one of the women's hands. "Join me," he ordered.

"I will... in a minute," the woman said.

"I wasn't asking," he said as his eyes glowed then slid her hand down his body to his hard cock. "Now, woman."

He then walked her off.

Meanwhile upstairs, Naheem and Ljerka, once again, lay in each other arms. Ljerka had a question she was burning to ask. As if sensing, Naheem started to roll onto his side facing her.

"Out with it," he ordered.

"Out with it, what?" she asked.

"Your question," he answered. "So, out with it."

"Fine," she said giving in. "Why am I here?"

"You came to me."

"I know but why?"

"I don't know." Lying to her.

"I dreamt of you before coming here."

"Hm," was all he said.

As if not hearing him, she continued. "It feels like we've been together before now."

I have, he thought. But not with you. Eve. They must be connected. He continued to hear her talk but really wasn't paying attention.

After a few moments, he said. "You talk to much. It's the Sin Festival. Let's Fuck." He kissed her stunned mouth. She was going to be a problem, he thought before his mind went blink.

Chapter 2

The next day, Ljerka woke up with a strange man in her bed. She looks around and realized it wasn't her room. She started to remember where she was and who she was with. Naheem. That was his name. He gave her the best five orgasms ever except for the one she had in her dream. She looks over at him. He's still sleeping, talking in his sleep.

"Eve. Eve," Naheem mumbles in his sleep.

"Whose Eve?" she whispers to herself.

Ljerka got up out the bed. She grabbed her robe and unlock the door. She snuck out the bedroom down the stairs and out the side door, they came in. She then ran down the street to the Inn. Who's Eve?

When the closed, Naheem woken up to a cold bed. He reached for Ljerka, but she was gone. "Shit!" he cursed punching a pillow. He then got up and put on his robe. She is just like Eve, he thought. Good with locks. This was the first time in years, he participated in the Sin Festival.

With Eve's sudden death, Naheem lost interest in the Festival. He never felt like participating until Ljerka came along. He got in the shower. He washed away the scent of sex and sleep. He couldn't believe he had five rounds in him. Thinking back made him hard. He stroked his cock to relive the pressure.

"Shit," he moans as he came.

This is going to be hard, he thought. Very hard.

Ljerka showered and dressed. Her pussy was sore from the night before, so she was careful. She grabbed her keys and jacket as she left her room. She then got in her rented car and drove off. She stopped at the lake just outside town. She got out of the car. She changed her shoes to walking sneakers then stretched. As she stretches, she heard feet behind her.

"I thought I was the only one that knew this place," a man's voice said.

"I guess I'm the second one, then," Ljerka said.

"Juliano O'Hara," Juliano introduced himself.

"Ljerka Tarrant," Ljerka introduces herself. "Nice to meet you."

"You too," Juliano said checking her out. "Did you enjoy the Sin Festival?"

She stiffened a little before she turned towards him. "Why do you ask?

"Just being friendly," he said.

"It was fine," not giving much away. "I got to go," then walked off.

"Enjoy tonight," he yelled

Turning back around. "What?!" she yelled.

"I said enjoy tonight!" he yelled.

"I will!" she yelled back then turned back around.

Ljerka walked away. As she walked, she started getting flashes of images. She wasn't sure they were hers or not. They were of two little girls or one. She couldn't tell the difference. She began to get dizzy. The images began to come quickly. So quickly, she fainted.

Ljerka felt someone trying to shake her a wake. A man's voice calling to her.

"Ma'am! Ma'am!" the man said. "Can you hear me?"

"Mmm," she moans. "Please, don't yell."

"I think she's fine," he said.

Ljerka opens her eyes. She sees a pair of hazel eyes looking back at her. She sat up and looked around her. She didn't recognize where she was.

"Where am I?" she asked.

"At the Underfield Spring House," the man said. "Juliano brought you here."

"Why would he bring me here?" she demanded. "Why not a hospital?"

"It's because I told him to bring you here," Naheem said. "And the nearest hospital is in Eastbington. That's about five hundred miles north of here. Underfield has medication for every ailment."

"I see," not believing a word he says.

"The people of Goldenleaf don't get sick," he added.

"I am not from Goldenleaf."

"I'm well aware of at that, Ljerka."

Ljerka began to stand up but was stopped by Naheem.

"Where do you think you're going?" he demanded.

"I'm leaving," she answered. "If you'll excuse me."

"I don't think so. You're staying right here."

"What about my car?"

"What about it?"

"I left it on the side of the road."

"Maxim go get..." Naheem ordered Maxim.

"Already took care of it, Naheem," Juliano said cutting in.

"See, all taken care of," Naheem said. "Lay back and rest."

"No, I should be going," Ljerka protested.

"All your things have been packed and brought here," he said.

"Why?" she demanded.

"Enough question. Rest."

"But..." getting dizzy again.

Looking concerned. "Lay back before you fall down," he ordered.

"I'm not going to..." and she fell.

Naheem helped Ljerka get back in bed. Took her sneakers and pulls the covers over her.

"Naheem!" Seija called. "What's this about..."

"Shh!" Naheem said walking over to Seija. "I know what you're going to say..."

"No, you don't..." she countered.

"You're going to say, I shouldn't have let her be brought here," he said. "I know but..."

"But nothing," she countered. "She needs to leave now. She..."

"Ljerka is not leaving. Not until she's better. She just fainted."

"I don't care, Naheem. She leaves and she's leaving right now."

"Seija, this is my house. She's not leaving and that's..."

"Enough!" Ljerka said from the bed. "You're making my head hurt."

"Sorry," Naheem apologized.

"And I'm leaving once I fell a bit better," she said.

"No, you're not," he countered. "You're staying and that's final."

Naheem then storms out the room. They heard the room next door close.

"Don't worry," Ljerka reassured Seija. "I'll be out of your hair soon."

Seija just left the room.

After, hours later, it was night not yet moonrise. Ljerka heard voices from downstairs. She got up and left the room to find out who was down there.

Once she got closer, she heard laughing and talking. She walked to the top of the stairs then looked down. She saw men and women naked in robes. Then she saw Naheem. He wore a thin, almost sheer, robe. He was with the woman named Seija, Juliano, Jaxon, and Maxim.

They must be close, she thought. The clock chimes. Moonrise, she then thought. Everyone then disrobes and picks a partner. She notices Seija grabs Juliano's hand and leads him away. Maxim nudges Naheem and points to Ljerka at the tops of the stairs.

Naheem's eyes glows. Somehow the look turns Ljerka on. They stripped their clothes as they walked towards each other.

Once they met each other in the middle of the room, he pulls her into his arms and kisses her. She wrapped her arms around him. He walks her to the nearest wall and put her against it. He enters her now wet pussy. She rides him as he pumps up into her. They continue to kiss until he pulls back.

"Open your eyes, Ljerka," Naheem ordered. "I want to see your eyes when I will fuck you."

Ljerka opens them and stares into Naheem's. Their eyes were glowing. There was pleasure and animal lust in them.

"Mmm...Aahhh," they both moaned.

"Fuck...F-F-fuck," she moans.

He continues to pump into her while everyone else moaned and fucked. They could hear none of them around them. The sexual energy was so thick, you could cut it with a knife.

They both climax.

"Aahh...Shit," Ljerka moans.

"Shit," Naheem moans.

He puts her down. He hears her feet hit the floor. He turns her around. Pressing her gently against the wall. Her hot cheek was pressed against the cold wall. She felt him smack her ass. She then felt him enter her pussy from behind.

"Mmm," she moans.

Naheem begins to move in and out of her. He moves fast and hard. He moans again. "Fuck!"

Ljerka moans and moves against him. "Aahh," she moans. She reaches behind her to grasp his hand.

They both climax. They scream out each other names. Naheem then pulled out of her and turns her back around. They kissed again.

"She definitely going to be trouble," she told woman next to her.

"I know," the other woman said. "We'll have to do something about it."

"We will after the...mmm...Sin Festival."

"It may be too late. Look at them."

The women looked them Ljerka and Naheem seemed like they were the only ones in the room. They watched them until Naheem walked her out the room.

"Definitely a problem," one of the women said.

"Definitely," the woman said.

Naheem walks Ljerka into the hall and up the stairs. Once at the tops, he walks her to a bathroom. He opens the door and pulls her inside. The jacuzzi tub was already filled. There were candles all around. He helped her into the bath then got in after her. He then moves towards her as she moves towards him.

With soap and bubbles everywhere, they kiss as Naheem enters her once again. They both moan in pleasure. Their slick bodies were wet. They ran their hands up and down their bodies.

Ljerka rode Naheem's cock. She held onto his shoulders as she did so. She feels her orgasm build as she felt him finger her clit.

"Aahhh," she moans against his lips.

They climaxed together.

Chapter 3

The next day, Ljerka left Underfield Spring House to go shopping for extra clothes. She saw a little boutique and walked inside. She looks around and picked out a few items. She walked to the register as she picked up a lipstick or two.

"Is that all today?" the boutique owner asked politely.

"Yes, for now," Ljerka answered putting her items on counter to be rung out.

"So, how are you liking Goldenleaf?" she then asked bagging Ljerka's items.

"I like it well enough," Ljerka said. "It's an interesting place."

"How so?" another man wondered.

"I don't know really," grabbing her bags. "I never been in town like this before. You put decorations of people in sex positions in all your windows."

"It's for..."

I know it'd for the Sin Festival but won't children see and ask question?" Ljerka asked.

"They do but we explain everything from an early age," Naheem explained from behind her.

"How young?" Ljerka demanded.

"Ten years old," he said.

"Ten years old? Ten years old?!" she said outraged. "You can't tell a ten years old about sex."

"We can and do," he said. "Our children are very mature."

"I see," she said. So, he had children, she thought.

Ljerka paid for items. She then grabbed her bags but before she could, Naheem got them. "I got them," she said.

"I know but I was being nice," he said.

They walked out of the boutique. Naheem walked Ljerka into the next shop. It was a...

"Lingerie?" she questioned. "I don't need..."

"Yes, you do," he countered. "You can't be naked all the time."

"Well if I was at the Inn, I can be naked in my room. I have a robe."

"I know but in my house, you need a modest robe. No just a see-through one."

"I have others. I packed two. The one the other night and a heavier one."

"Well, I'll get you another."

"I don't need another... Wait, your home?"

"Yes, I own Underfield Spring House."

"What?! Why didn't you tell me?"

"It didn't come up. I had my mind on other things, Ljerka."

"You still should have..."

"How? Before or after our rows of sex!" he almost yelled.

People in the shop stared their way.

"Shh," Ljerka said. "Not so loud."

"Why not?" Naheem demanded. "Everyone saw us having sex."

"I don't care," she snapped. "I'm leaving."

"Where are you going?" he asked changing his tone.

"I'm going back home. I can't find what I'm looking for."

"What are you looking for, Ljerka?"

"Trying to locate and family of mine that's living. I was..." she stops talking takes her bags from Naheem. "It's none of your business. Just know, I'm leaving."

"Okay." Standing there as she leaves. He then takes out her cellphone. He takes out his own. "Jaxon, make sure Ljerka doesn't leave... I'll explain later... I know she isn't Eve... Just do it," then hung up.

Naheem grabbed and picked up the robe for Ljerka before leaving the store.

"You can't leave, Ljerka," Jaxon said. "Naheem said…"

"Fuck what Naheem said," Ljerka cursed. "I'm leaving."

"If she wants to leave, let her," Seija said. "Move out the way," she ordered.

"I can't do that, Seija," he said. "Not even for you."

"Oh really," she sneered. She was up to Jaxon and flirted a little. She then whispers something in his ear.

Ljerka watches Seija flirt to get Jaxon to do what she wants. She was succeeding until Naheem came through the front door.

"Shit!" Seija cursed before walking away from, a cock hardened, Jaxon.

"Nice try, sister dear," Naheem to Seija then to Ljerka. "You can't leave," putting down the shopping bag. "You can't miss the last night of the Sin."

"I don't care about the Sin Festival, Naheem," Ljerka said. "I want to go home."

"But you are home, Ljerka," he said.

"What are you…I'm home?! How?"

"This isn't the time to be telling her…" Seija scolded. "The family…"

"What family?' Ljerka demanded.

"It's not important," Seija said.

"If it has to do with me, it is," Ljerka said.

"I think it's time to tell her," Naheem said. "but slowly."

"Stop talking around me!" Ljerka yelled. "And tell me what family."

"It's not…" Naheem's sister started to say.

"Shut up!" Ljerka and Naheem yelled in unison.

"And you," Ljerka said talking to Naheem. "Talk. Spill. Now!"

"Seija, can you…" he requested.

"Sure," his sister said giving in. "You'll regret it, dear brother." Leaving the room.

"What did she mean by that, Naheem?" Ljerka demanded.

"It's nothing, Ljerka," Naheem said.

"He's telling her right now," Seija said to another woman on the phone.

"What?!" another woman demanded. "You should have..."

"I know, Enis," she said "But..."

"But nothing, Enis said. "We got to get rid of Eve for a reason."

"I know."

"We can't have her knowing about Eve. Not yet anyway."

Ljerka was yelling in the background on Seija's side of the phone.

"I guess she knows not," Enis said. "Damn it! I'll be right over."

"Alright," Seija sighed.

They both hung up.

"What do you mean my twin sister, I never knew about, is dead?" Ljerka demanded.

"I'm sorry, Ljerka," Naheem said.

"And she was your wife," she said angrily. "Why did you fuck me?"

"Eve was my wife, yes," he said. "but...'

"I reminded you of her. That's no..."

Two children ran to Naheem. One of them, the girl, looked just like child version of Ljerka. She had the same face, nose, mouth. Everything was the same. The little boy looks like Naheem. Ljerka just looked a at them in shocked.

"Daddy!" they squealed and gripped both his legs.

"Hey, Rina," Naheem said to the girl. And to the boy. "Hey, Levi." Giving a kiss on the forehead.

"Daddy, who's that?" Rina asked.

"She looks like mommy," Levi added.

"Well..." their father was about to say.

"I am your Auntie Ljerka," Ljerka answered. "Your mom was my twin sister."

"But mom said..." Rina started to say turning to her father.

"I know what mommy said," Naheem interrupted her. "I guess she didn't know. Your auntie came to visit."

"And now I'm leaving," Ljerka added turning to go to the door.

As she made her way to the door. Someone pulled at her bag. She looks back, Rina was behind her.

"Hi, I'm Katharina," Rina said introducing herself. "Why are you leaving?"

"I shouldn't have come here," Ljerka said. "I found out what I was looking for. It's time to go."

"My mom died," was all she said letting Ljerka's bag go. "I miss her."

"I know, Katharina, but I can't..."

"I know you can't, but can we get your phone number to call you?"

"I don't think that's a good idea, honey," feeling sorry for the girl.

Ljerka left. She put everything she bagged and bought in the back seat and trunk of the car. She got behind the wheel. Started the car and drove off. She stops just outside Goldenleaf. She puts the car in park and gets out. She then looks out on the water.

So, Eve is my twin sister, she thought. She has two children, twins, with Naheem. Who she had the best sex and five orgasm with? Wow, what a town.

Ljerka's phone rang it was Taiki.

"Hello?" she answered.

"Ljer, I just go your phone call," Taiki said. "Sorry, I didn't answer. I turned my phone off at work."

"That's okay."

"Wait, you didn't chew me out. What's wrong?"

"I'll tell you when I get home."

"Home? I thought you'd be staying another month."

"Things change, Taiki. Plus, I found what I was looking for."

"Something happened. Tell me."

"I will when I get home. There's a lot to tell."

"Then start now."

Ljerka paused for a moment. "Okay," giving in. "Where you want me to start?"

"The beginning is a good start," Taiki said.

"I have an identical twin sister named Eve."

"You have a twin," she repeated after Ljerka.

"Yes, that's not the end of it…Eve is married to a man named Naheem. Who I fucked and they have twins a boy and a girl?"

"Wait a minute, you fucked your sister's husband?"

"Yes, I did. Oh, I forgot to tell you she died."

"She died but how?"

"Eve died in an accident suddenly."

"Why did you fuck with your dead sister's husband?"

"First off, I thought he was single. No ring. Second off, it was part of the Sin festival."

"Sin Festival, what is that?"

"The Sin Festival is a big festival with people having sex. It's only happened in Goldenleaf, T. Get this… they tell the children about sex at ten. Also, they hang up decoration of sex positions in their windows."

"What?! No! Why?"

"You don't want to know."

"Okay what else?"

"That's pretty much it. Oh. One more thing."

"What's that?"

"Naheem's sister, Seija, doesn't like me."

"His sister doesn't like you, why?"

"I don't know, T, and I don't care. I'm coming home."

"Alright. One last question…"

"What is it?"

"What other family do you have there? Other than the brother-in-law and nieces and nephews."

"I don't know.

Chapter 4

"So, she left," Seija said. "Good. There won't be no more problems."

"Seija, what do you mean by that?" Naheem demanded.

"Well, she was..." she drifted off.

"Trouble but for who?" he demanded. "For you and your little friends."

"Not...'

"I knew you and your friends did something to make her leave."

"Could it have been the information you didn't tell her about?"

"Or it be because you wanted her gone?"

"Either way, I'm happy she's gone."

"Well, I'm not, Seija," he left the room.

"Shit!" she cursed.

After weeks later, Ljerka began working from home. She was like a moody zombie. Snapping at her friends, co-workers, and family, she was adopted into. Only Taiki knew what was going with Ljerka.

"You need to cut everyone some slack, Ljer," Taiki ordered. "They love you. They're not like the people of Goldenleaf."

"I know that, T," Ljerka snapped. Calming down. "I know but I miss..."

"Yes, I know," Taiki said. "Let's go out," she suggested.

"Can't."

"Why not?"

"Because I'm busy with work. I'm so behind, T."

"I'll tell the boss you needed a night out."

"But you're the boss, T."

"I know. So, I'm giving you the night off. It's Friday come on, Ljer. We'll have drinks and hit on cute guys."

"Okay but not Lucky's. Let's try some place new."

"Some place new. No Lucky's. Deal?"

"Deal."

Ljerka and Taiki dressed in black slimming dresses. Ljerka was trimmed in red and Taiki was trimmed in heather grey. They walked into the club called Climax. Climax, they came to find out was an underground sex club.

"Are you sure you want to go there?" Taiki asked.

"I'm sure," Ljerka answered. "Very sure," before going inside as the bouncer held the door open. She had to pull Taiki inside behind her.

Inside Climax, people made out and were having sex. The two women walked around until they were greeting by the host and hostess.

"Hello," they greeted them.

"You must be new," the woman said.

"Yes, we are," Ljerka said as her glowing eyes flickered like a dying light bulb. She was getting horny off the scent of sex.

"Come," the man ordered. "We'll find some gentlemen for you."

"By the way, I'm Ilia," the woman introduced herself. "And this is Felip," pointing at the man next to her.

"I'm Ljerka," Ljerka introduced herself. "And this is Taiki," pointing at Taiki.

Felip left them to bring over two men. Both had dreads and tattoos.

"Omar. Alonzo meet Taiki and Ljerka," Felip said introducing them. "Make these ladies comfortable."

"Yes, sir," the men said.

Omar took Ljerka by the hand as Alonzo took Taiki's. They walked them to private room right next to each other. The rooms had king size beds in them. Omar and Alonzo walks Taiki and Ljerka to the bed. They start kissing as the women rubs against them. The men slid their hands up and down the women bodies.

Taiki stopped Alonzo. "I can't do this," leaving the room. She knocks on the door which Ljerka was in with Omar. "Ljerka, I can't do this."

The door opens, Ljerka peeks out. She was half dressed. Her eyes were glowing. She felt Omar pull her panties aside and enter her wet pussy. "Mmm," she moans. "What...can't you do?"

"This," Taiki answered. "I can't do this, Ljerka. No offense, Alonzo."

"None taken," Alonzo said walking away. "Shit!" He cursed under his breath.

Taika didn't hear him but still felt bad. "I'm going. See you at home," leaving the doorway.

"Wait, I'll be right behind you," Ljerka said closing the door. "I have to go," she said reluctantly to Omar.

"I heard," Omar said pulling out of her.

She moved around the room. She grabs her purse, coat, and shoes. She takes out a card and wrote her phone number down. She gave him one last kiss. "Call me," then left the room to join Taiki.

At their apartment, Ljerka and Taiki walked in arguing.

"I can't believe you like that place Climax," Taiki argued. "It was a sex club."

"I was curious, T," Ljerka argued. "Climax seemed like a cool place to hang out."

"A sex club, Ljer? A sex clubs?!"

"Yes, I guessed wrong for you, then."

"Un huh, you did...Ever since you came from Goldenleaf, you came back a different person."

"I know," she agreed. "But after participating in the Sin Festival, you would too."

"Yea, but a sex club? Next time, you go by yourself. Also, why were your eyes glowing?"

"I don't know really. I just noticed it happens when I'm horny. It happened a lot in Goldenleaf."

"Did you ask why?"

"No." The phone rings. She searched her purse. Once she found it, Ljerka answered. She grinned at the voice. "Hey Omar..."

"You gave Omar your number?!" Taiki asked shocked. "Why... Never mind," walking away. "We'll talk later."

A few hours later, Omar was knocking at Ljerka and Taiki's apartment door. Ljerka answered it.

"Hey," she greeted him with just a robe on.

"Hey," he greeted her looking her up and down. "Mm. Mm. Mm." walking inside.

Ljerka kiss Omar as she closes the door. She walks him to her bedroom. Once inside, she undressed him. She unbuttoned his shirt and pants, then opens his shirt and kiss down his well muscled body. She stops at his pants and then down boxers and all.

Omar just stood there in utter pleasure. He then her slides his cock in her mouth and let her suck it. He moans in pleasure and rocked against it. He gripped her hair.

She sucks him until he's hard. Then stands up and kiss him. She feels him turn and walk her to the bed.

They tumble onto the bed. Omar rises above her and undo her robe. He kissed her neck then down her body. He stops at her legs as they opened for him. He then knelt between them and opened her pussy lips to suck and tongue flick her clit. She moans as she feels a finger enter her. She feels it go in and out, in and out.

Ljerka feels her first orgasm build and build. "Aahh...Mmm...Aahh...Shit," she moans again pleasure. She climaxes. "Aahh," she moans again as she arches like a bow.

Just as she's coming down, he enters her fast. He pumps into her hard and fast. They both moans. She wraps her arms and legs around him. She moves her hips up to meet him stroke for stroke.

"Aahh...Naheem!" Ljerka screams in pleasure.

"Aahh," Omar screams in pleasure. He hears her call out another man's name. "Shit!" he then said pulling out of her.

Naheem was never the same after Ljerka left. He was moody and he always brooded. When the Sin Festival came around, he fucked random women to get Ljerka out of his mind.

"It's not the same," he thought aloud. He saw bits and pieces of Ljerka, and Eve, in every woman he was with.

Naheem called out either Eve or Ljerka name during his climaxes. The women don't mind. They were happy he picked them because he was the Master of the Sin Festival. He was named that because of the pleasure he gave his sex partners.

One day, Naheem was playing with Katharina and Levi when the phone rang. He ignored it. The phone continued to ring.

"Are you going to get that," Seija demanded.

"No, I'm busy," Naheem answered.

"Too busy to answer the phone." Answering the phone. "Hello...yes...So, you found her...I'll tell him...Bye," she hangs up. "They found Ljerka. She's in Eastborne Falls."

"Okay," Naheem said. "Good to know."

"Yeah," Seija said then walked off.

Naheem stopped playing with her children. They looked confused. "Daddy has to go out of town."

"Aww. Why?" Katharina and Levi asked.

"I have to take care of something," he answered.

"Is it about the phone call you got?" Katharina asked.

Rina takes after her mother, he thought. Smart as a whip. "Yes, Rina." Her father said.

Rina let him go at the same time as her twin brother. "Off you go," Rina said.

Her mother's daughter, he thought nodding getting up and walking away. He packed his clothes as he called someone to bring his car around. Once he was done, he went to first door. Jaxon grabbed Naheem's bags and put them in the car.

"What are you going to do when you find her?" Jaxon asked.

"I don't know. Probably bring her back," Naheem answered. "Take care of Rina and Levi." Getting behind the wheel.

Before he could close the door, Jaxon stopped him. "Are you sure you should be doing this?"

"Yes, I am," Naheem reassured him. "I'm really sure." Then closed the door and drive off.

Once on the open rode, Naheem was trying to clear his head. He had the windows down and the wind was blowing steady. He put his windows up to use his car phone.

"Hello, I'm Naheem Lukas. I need to find a room in Eastborne Falls...Yes, one person...No, it doesn't matter...Okay...I'll be there by about 4:30 tonight...All right, thank you... yes...Bye," then he hung up.

At about four o'clock, Naheem arrived in Eastbourne Falls. He drove around to get the feel of the city. So, Ljerka came from here, he thought. Not a bad place. He then drove to his hotel to sign in and go to his room to rest.

At about six that night, Ljerka was laying in bed when Omar got up to leave. This was the Seventh time they had sex, but he was the same as Naheem. She had been dreaming about him a lot lately and didn't know why. She felt like he was close, but he was in Goldenleaf, wasn't he?

As Naheem settled in his room, he called room service for the nearest specialty club. They didn't know what he was talking about. It guesses they don't know what specialty clubs are, he thought. He decided to drive around.

He got in his car and drove around. His phone car phone rang.

"Hello?"

"Hey, this is Jerome Foguer. Private investigator. I see you got my call since you're in town."

"Yes, I did," Naheem said. "Why are you call me now?"

"To fill you in," Jerome answered. "To tell you what your little lady friend been up to."

"Why?"

"You need to know. Meet my at Climax."

"Climax? Why there?"

"My lead was last there."

"All right. Be there in ten."

Yea." Jerome said then hung up.

Ten minutes later, Naheem was parking and getting out. He met Jerome at the door. "So, why did you want to meet me here?"

"This is the place she was last before she went home. She got a call from this place everyday this week," Jerome informed him.

"And so," was all Naheem said.

"Follow me." Then walked inside once the bouncer let them in.

Naheem was in shock somewhat. His eyes started flicking. The aroma of sex was thick as jello or even thick or something thicker than that. Fuck, he thought. His cock was getting hard just standing in there. He took out his sunglasses and put them on.

"As you can see, Ljerka came and got called from a sex club," Jerome said. "Do you think..."

"I don't know," Naheem said but he did know. She was looking for some connection to Goldenleaf's Sin Festival. Damn and she don't know what she was. "Shit!" then turned to leave.

"Where you going?" Jerome demanded. "Where do you..."

Naheem didn't answer. He just walked faster out of Climax. He walked to his car and got in. A few seconds later, Jerome tapped at his car window. It startled him but he rolled down the window. "Yeah,"

"I have her home address." Jerome said then handing him a piece of paper.

"Thanks," taking the paper and rolled up the window.

Jerome moved back as Naheem started the car. He watched him pulled off.

Chapter 5

Ljerka was relaxing in her bathtub when the doorbell rang. Taiki yelled and said she'd get it. Ljerka was falling a sleep when Taiki knocked on the bathroom door.

"Yeah?" Ljerka answered.

"The door is for you," Taiki yelled from the other side of the door.

"Who would come here this late?" she asked.

"I don't know, Ljer. All I know is he asked for you by name," the other woman said. "He also that he's an old friend from Goldenleaf."

"Fine, I'll be right there." So, Naheem found me, she thought. Well damn. It was fun while it lasted.

Ljerka got out the tub and dried off. She walked to her room and put on the heaviest robe she had and her house shoes. She went down to the living room. She heard voices talking. She stood in the doorway.

"So, you found me," Ljerka said to Naheem.

Naheem turned around. "I guess I did," he said. "You're a hard lady to find. There are four other people with your name."

"I see," was all that she said.

Before she could continue, Taiki asked. "Is that Mr. Five Orgasm?"

"Taiki, can we have a minute?" Ljerka countered not answering her friend's question.

"Okay," Taiki said. "Nice meeting you."

"You too, Taiki," Naheem said back to her.

Taiki walked off leaving them a lone.

"So..." Ljerka started to say.

"So..." Repeated after her.

"Naheem, what are you doing here?" she asked.

"Well Ljerka, I'm here because you left after I asked you to say," he answered.

"You demanded I stayed..."

"I didn't demand..."

"Yes, you did. After you told your sister, I was to stay. I stayed long enough to know I slept with a married man."

"I'm a widower, Ljerka, for close to three years now."

"Did you ever find out what happened to her, my sister?"

"No, it went unsolved. It's a cold case."

"And since I look so much like her, you have sex with me."

"No, it wasn't meant to be like that...actually, it was like that, but I wasn't thinking of Eve in any way."

"The hell you weren't! The first night of the Sin Festival, you moaned Eve's name in your sleep."

"Well..."

"You were thinking of her." Not letting him talk. "You can leave now!" walking to the door.

"Damn it, will you let me talk?" he demanded. "That night I did dream of Eve," he began.

"I knew..."

"But I was having a nightmare of her death again. They had stopped before you came to town."

"So, you're trying to say I'm giving you nightmares of my sister. Hm."

"You can ask my sister Seija about them. I'll call her now."

"No, maybe tomorrow. It's late, Naheem. What do you want anyway?"

"You, for starters." When Ljerka's left brow raised, he then changed his tune. "But I'll stop while I'm ahead."

"Naheem, I still need answers." Walking away from the door to the couch then padded the seat next to her.

"What you want to know?" sitting next to her.

"Too many questions."

"Start with me one you've been burning to ask."

"While, I want to know why my eyes glow during sex and when I'm horny. Also, who is my family?"

Looking at his clock and seeing the time. "We'll have to wait on that for right now."

"But..."

"Tomorrow. I'll buy you lunch."

"Why did you just do that?" she demanded."

"It's moonrise. Happy Sin Festival."

"Huh?! Your eyes are all ready flickering."

She got up to look in the small mirror over the couch. "Why do they do that?"

"Okay, I'll answer this one," giving in. He couldn't deny her anything.

"Tell me,"

"Well, all the people of Goldenleaf have eyes that do that. We come from a species that have people that have eyes that glow when aroused or when we are horny. During the Sin Festival every weekend, we satisfy our urges."

The whole time Naheem talked, he pulled the rope on Ljerka's robe and opened it. He them slide a finger down her breasts. Down to her naval then to between her legs. She opened her legs to him. He kissed her neck when he was done talking.

"So, you're telling me... I'm some kind of... mmm...creature that have eyes that glow and that's horny all the time?"

"Mm Hm," he said.

"Damn," was all she said. "What about my family?"

"Shh, later. Later." Then he kissed her lips.

Naheem swept her into his arms. "Where is your bedroom?"

"Upstairs. First door on the right," Ljerka moaned.

He went up the stairs and to the first room on the right. He opened the door, went inside and kicked it close. He then walked over to the bed and laid her on the bed. He climbed into of her and continued to kiss down her body once again. He hears her moan and moan.

When they were burning with need, Ljerka felt Naheem enter her wet pussy. "Aahh," she moans. He moans a long with her. He pumped into her slowly as she moaned for him to go faster. He promised himself he would go slow when he saw her again.

It was killing him that he was going that slow but, he had to prove he could go slow and not be so urgent.

"Damn it, Naheem, go faster!" Ljerka demanded. "Go faster!"

Naheem just ignored her and went the pace he planned. When she didn't quiet down, he kissed her. He broke long enough to kiss her neck. He felt kiss the skin right behind his ear and he just lost it.

"Fuck!" he moaned then pumped into her fast and hard.

"Finally! Yes!" then she moaned. "Aahh!"

Naheem chuckled and rolled over onto his back. "Ride me," he ordered.

Ljerka sat up and ride him fast and hard. She felt his hands on either side of her hips. "Aahh...Shittt!" she moans a loud. She hears him moan and sat up. She kisses him. Tongues intertwine as moans sounded.

They were so loud, it woke Taiki up. She just cursed and turned over. When they wouldn't quiet down, she got up and banged on Ljerka's door. When that didn't work, she opened the door and got a full view.

"Oh my gosh!" Taiki said in shock.

They didn't even stop. Didn't even flitch. They were so absorbed in each other that they even know Taiki was in the doorway.

"Oh my gosh!" she repeated then tried to look away but couldn't.

Naheem and Ljerka changed positions once more. They moved into the doggy style. He enters her wet pussy once more. He smacked her ass and continued to pump her fast and hard.

"Aahh...Mmm...Aahh," they moaned in unison.

Taiki watched and watched. She was just planted in place. She was getting hot and horny just looking at them. Damn, she thought. They have me so...Mmm. Damn. She then walked out the room. "Damn it!" she said.

Chapter 6

"Wow," was all Ljerka could say moments later.

"I know right," Naheem agreed.

"That was...Wow," she said.

She got up and noticed the door was open. "When did..." Naheem shrugged his shoulders. "Never mind," she said.

She walked out the door and saw Taiki's room empty. She then wondered door stairs and saw her room mate in the living room watching television. She went in the room and peered inside to see what she was watching.

"Everything is okay, T?" Ljerka asked.

Taiki jumped and shut off the television. "So, you two are done, I see?"

"Yeah, but why are you up so early?" She wondered.

"Couldn't sleep," was all her room mate said.

"Sorry if we were too loud but it gets that way with us," apologizing to Taiki.

"I never knew it could be like that."

"Me neither."

"Does he have a brother?" Taiki chuckled.

"When he gets up, I'll find out."

"When who gets up?" Naheem asked walking into the living room.

Ljerka and Taiki both jump and turn towards the doorway.

"Taiki was asking if you have a brother?" Ljerka asked him.

"Ljer, why did you..." Taiki demanded.

"You wanted to know, didn't you?"

"Well yeah but you didn't have to ask in front of me."

"Ladies, it is fine you asked because I was just going to ask if you, Taiki, wanted to visit Goldenleaf? You killed two birds with one stone so to speak."

"Sure. Okay, thank you, Naheem is it?"

"Yes, it is," Naheem said. "I better be going. I was away from my hotel room long enough. I need a little sleep before my drive home."

"Why did you get a hotel room for?" Ljerka asked. "There is plenty of room here... Wait, drive home?"

"Yes, drive home. I can't stay, Ljerka. I have a business to run," he explained. "And if I stayed here, I wouldn't want to leave."

"Oh, okay but what time are you going to leave?" Taiki asked.

"T?!" Ljerka scolded.

"I know it shouldn't have came out like that but I need to know," Ljerka's room mate said. "I need to make plans and push back meeting."

"But you're the boss, T," Ljerka said.

"Yeah, I know," grabbing her cell. " I'll make some calls."

"I'll walk you to the door," to Naheem.

Ljerka walked Naheem to the front door. He kissed her goodbye then left.

Naheem made some calls of his own. He called his brother, Kamal, and told him there was a guest coming with Ljerka when he came back home. He entered his hotel room and went to the bathroom to shower. He washed off the sweatiness of last night sex. That last kiss he gave almost killed him. He didn't want to leave but for himself and her, he did.

Later that week, Ljerka And Taiki worked to get ready for there trip to Goldenleaf. That Thursday, they packed their bags. The next day, they took their bags and put them in Ljerka's trunk. Taiki followed Naheem's car to Goldenleaf.

"That bitch is coming back," Seija said.

"I thought we was rid of her," her friend said.

"She's coming back and she is bringing a friend for Kamal."

"Ugh! Shit!"

"Can't believe he's went to find her."

"What! Why didn't Naheem didn't say anything?" her friend demanded.

"It wasn't none of our business, they said."

"What?! So, we'll have to get rid of them, too."

"Basically."

Naheem, Ljerka, and Taiki made it to Goldenleaf around six in the afternoon. They drive to Underfield Spring House and was greeted by Jaxon and Juliano at the door. Naheem parked and let Ljerka out while Jaxon let Taiki.

"Wow," Taiki shocked looking up at the house.

"I know right," Ljerka agreed. "That's what I felt when I first saw it." Walking over towards her friend.

"My brother, Kamal, has a similar house called the Underfield Autumn house on the other side the town," Naheem informed them.

"Why didn't you tell me?" Ljerka demanded.

"Because I want you all to myself." Walking over to kiss Ljerka's lips.

"Aww, nice try," chuckling after elbowing him in his side.

All he did was chuckle. "Jaxon, help me with their bags."

"Yes sir," Jaxon said. "I'll take them to their rooms."

"Thanks, Jax," Naheem thanked him.

They carried the bags into the foyer and went upstairs to the two guest rooms. Ljerka went in the bedroom next to Naheem and Taiki was put the room down the hall away from their rooms.

Someone rang the doorbell, Juliano answered it. It was Kamal so he let him in.

"I'll get Naheem for you," Juliano said heading upstairs.

"Thank you, Juls," Kamal thanked him.

Kamal stood in the foyer when a woman came down the stairs. One he never seen. He looked her up and down. Who was she? He thought. She's hot.

"Do you know where the kitchen is?" she asked.

"Yes, I'll show you," he said walking a head of her leaving her to follow.

Before they walked into the kitchen, Naheem and Ljerka walked down the stairs.

"Taiki, I guess I don't have to introduce you to my brother, Kamal." Naheem said.

"Your brother, Kamal, "Ljerka said. "You two look nothing a like."

"Thank you, I think," Kamal chuckled. "So, this is Ljerka. She looks just Eve."

"Kam, seriously?" Naheem scolded. "That's a sore topic."

"I didn't know," Kamal said.

"Sorry to interrupt but I'm hungry," Taiki said. "And Kamal, is it?" Kamal nodded his head. "Kamal was just showing me the kitchen."

"We were just going out to eat," Naheem informed her. "We were just about to get you."

"Eat out where?" Taiki asked.

"There are a few places in town that has good food," Kamal said.

"Is there a decent grocery store in town?" Taiki asked.

"There's two," Kamal informed her. "...at either side of town."

"Okay, let's go there and I'll buy some food to cook," Taiki said.

"You're going to cook and you're the guest?" Kamal and Naheem asked.

"Yes, I do," she answered.

"She likes to cook," Ljerka informed. "No matter if she's a guest."

"I see," Kamal said, liking her all ready. "I'll take you, then." Taking out his car keys.

"All right, thanks," Taiki thanked him. "I'll get my wallet."

She went upstairs and got her wallet. They both left in Kamal's car.

Chapter 7

Kamal drove Taiki to the grocery store closest to Naheem's house. Kamal parked the car and got out to her help Taiki out. They walked into the grocery store and Taiki got a cart.

"You don't have to go with me, Kamal," Taiki said.

"I was going to help with the heavy things," Kamal said.

"I'm fine," She reassured him. "You can go off if you have to."

"No, I'm fine," he said. "Curious about what's for dinner."

"Oh. I'm making goulash. My version anyway."

"Yum. That's my favorite dish."

"Good. I'm making it with garlic and cheese bread and veggies."

"Damn. I hope it's tastes as good as it sounds."

"It does. Just ask Ljerka. She didn't have any complaints."

"Good. You probably won't get any from Heem and I, also."

"All righty, then."

"Where to first?"

"Produce," she said. "Then the meat section."

"Okay," he said.

Kamal and Taiki stayed in the grocery store for about an hour or so. Taiki bought about $90 worth of food. Kamal helped her put the bags of groceries in the back seat and trunk of his car. Kamal then drove to the nearest liquor store and got out.

Thirty minutes later, Kamal came out and got in the car. He handed Taiki the bottle. He then started the car and drove back to Naheem's house.

Meanwhile at Naheem's house, Naheem and Ljerka were making out on his couch when they heard Kamal's car honk. They paused their kissing to see who was outside.

"Shit!" they both cursed.

"They just had to come back now," Ljerka said and Naheem nodding in agreement.

Naheem pulled Ljerka up from the couch and he got up. They walk hand and hand to the kitchen door. Once they were outside, they helped with the bags.

"What all did you get?" Naheem demanded bring in the last of the bags.

"Food," Taiki answered taking out the food from the bags.

"Why so much?" he then asked.

Looking at the items her friend was taking out. "Noo, I know you're not making it," Ljerka said.

"I am," Taiki confirmed. "Where are your pots and pans?"

"What is she making?" Naheem demanded taking out the pots and pans.

"She's making goulash. Her version of it," Kamal answered his brother.

"What?!" Naheem shocked putting them on the counter.

"Yes, goulash," Taiki confirmed. "You have a problem with that?"

"No," he said. "It's actually my favorite."

"All right. Good," Ljerka's friend said. "Give me the kitchen. Everyone out." Pushing them towards the door leading to the living room and dining room.

Everyone left but Kamal. He lingered and leaned against the counter, watching her.

"You need to go, too," Taiki ordered.

"No," Kamal said.

"No? I don't like people in my kitchen when I cook," she said moving around.

"This is not your kitchen," he clarified. "It's my brother's."

"I know that," turning to the stove and turning on the eye. "But when I'm using this kitchen it's mine."

"Fine but I think I'll stay. Put me to work."

"Fine," matching his tone. "Cut up the onion and bell pepper." Then put a big frying pan on it.

Taiki pointing to them while she got the ground beef, ground turkey, and sausage. She unpackaged them and put the pan. She got the wooden spoon and stirred it around until they were brown.

"Like this?" Kamal asked showing her.

"Yes, but a little smaller," she said. "Like this." Going over and showing him.

She guided her hands around his. Hmm, Taiki thought. He smells so good.

Damn, Kamal thought. I can't wait to...

"Kamal," she called. "Kamal..."

He had to shake that thought from his mind. "Yea! Yes," he said.

"This is the size I want." pointing down at the counter.

Kamal looks down and nods his head. "All right." Getting on with the cutting.

Taiki went back to browning the meat. Once she was done, she took it out then took the peppers and onions from Kamal. "Open the cans for me, too," she ordered.

"All right," he said. He got the cans and the can opener.

As Kamal opened the cans, he watched Taiki. The Sin Festival was in a few hours. He couldn't wait to spend it with Taiki. She was his kind of woman. He hoped she was good in bed.

Taiki felt Kamal looking at her. She didn't like and it was making her nervous. She rounded her shoulders and tried to ignore him.

"Something where?" Kamal wondered.

"No," she answered continued rounding her shoulders.

"You keep rounding your shoulders," he noticed.

Kamal finished opening the cans and goes to stand behind her and massage her shoulders. "Relax," he ordered when she tensed under his hand.

Taiki tried to relax but couldn't. He was making her aroused when she was trying to focus on cooking and couldn't. Damn, she thought. He needs to stop, or I'll burn this food. "Could you, please, stop?" she asked politely.

"Why?" he asked. "Am I making you uncomfortable?" starting to kiss her neck. "Good."

"Mmm," she moans. "I need to finish this food."

"So, finish it." Holding her waist.

"So, when is the goulash going to be done?" Naheem asked from the doorway.

Taiki jumped and tried to move away from Kamal but he kept his hands on her waist. "It should be done soon."

Naheem looked from Taiki to Kamal and back again. He then nodded and left for the living room.

Taiki blushed as she made the sauce. She watched Kamal pass her the open cans. He never let her go. She emptied the cans contains into the large pot. She rinsed out the cans and poured the extra sauce in the pot.

She tried to move away from him, but he was right with her.

"Can you get the macaroni for me, please?" she asked.

Kamal reached for the macaroni then handed it to her. "All of them?" she nodded yes. "Okay," he handed her the two packages.

"Thank you," she thanked him filling up another big pot with water.

She then put it on the stove and turning it on.

Naheem and Ljerka sat on the couch. They didn't turn the television. He told her about her family. He promised to bring her by their house tomorrow. She agreed.

"What are there names?" Ljerka asked.

"Dovie and Marty Hegarty. They own the shop next to mine," Naheem answered.

"That book shop?" she asked.

"Yes," he said. "Mmm, that goulash smells good."

"I Know right. I'm surprised that Taiki let Kamal stay in the kitchen with her."

"Why you say that?"

"She doesn't like people in her kitchen no matter if it's someone else's kitchen."

"Interesting."

"How so?"

"Kamal is the same way."

Taiki finished the goulash ten minutes later. "Can you tell Ljerka and Naheem the goulash is ready?"

"Okay," Kamal said leaving her alone.

Chapter 8

Ljerka, Kamal, Naheem, and Taiki sat at the small dining room table in the house. Taiki with Ljerka's help 'her put the food on the table. After the food was on the table, Taiki then dished up helpings for everyone. Naheem and Kamal took the first bite, they didn't stop eating until they were finished. They had two big helpings before they slowed down.

"They must like it," Ljerka chuckled eating.

"Good," Taiki said eating.

"Very good," Kamal said.

"Yes, very good," Naheem agreed.

"What smells so good?" Seija asked coming in the dining room.

"Goulash," was all Kamal said before taking another bite.

"Nooo, really?" his sister asked.

"Really," Naheem answered. "Taiki made it."

Seija helped herself to a helping of it. She tastes it. "Oh my gosh! This is great."

"I know right," Ljerka said. "Taiki cooking is great."

Seiji moaned in pleasured as she ate. The men did, too.

A few hours later, the five of them sat drinking wine. Seija left to meet up with her husband and bring him some goulash. Eventually, the men got up to put the food Taiki cooked.

"So, how you like Kamal?" Ljerka wondered.

"He's nice. A little..." Taiki started to say before the men comes back in.

They went to sit next to Taiki and Ljerka. They turned on the television and watched a movie. Halfway through the movie, Ljerka and Taiki falls a sleep. Kamal and Naheem carries them upstairs to their rooms. Kamal wanted to take Taiki to his house but couldn't.

The next day, Taiki and Ljerka woke up to find the men in the bed with them. Ljerka didn't mind but Taiki did because she didn't know Kamal well enough. She jumped out of bed and when into Ljerka's room. She noticed Naheem with her.

"Shit," Taiki cursed then left and went back to her room.

When she went inside, Kamal had woken up and saw her come in.

"Where did you go?" Kamal asked.

"No where," Taiki lied and had feeling that he knew she was lying.

"Okay," was all Kamal said. "I guess you are a little freaked out that I'm in the same bed as you."

"Yes," she said. "I was."

"I couldn't make it home last night, so I stayed. Before that you and Ljerka fell a sleep," he explained. Taiki just stared at him not believing him. "I see you don't believe me. We could ask Naheem when he gets up."

Taiki nodded. "Okay," staying where she was.

A few moments later, Naheem and Ljerka woke up. They heard talking. Ljerka got and put her robe on to check on her friend. She walked to Taiki's bedroom and looked inside. Taiki was standing a foot away from the bed talking to Kamal, where he lay.

"Everything okay, T?" Ljerka asked.

Taiki jumped and turned around. "Yes," She lied.

"No," Kamal said. "She thinks..."

"You don't know what I think, Kamal," Taiki countered.

"Yes, I sort of do," He countered. Then spoke to Ljerka. "Taiki seems to think I took advantage of her because I'm sleeping in the same bed as her."

"Didn't you?" Taiki demanded of him.

"I didn't and there was no where else to sleep," Kamal said.

"You could have slept on the floor," Taiki countered.

They continued to argue.

"Naheem!" Ljerka yelled. "Can you come here a minute?

Naheem came strolling in a few moments later. "Yea?"

Kamal saw his brother in the doorway. "Bro, tell them I didn't do anything to Taiki. I just brought her upstairs."

"He slept in the same as me," Taiki explained. "He could've taken the floor."

"Bad knees," the brothers' said in unison.

"He could of took the couch then," Taiki argued. "Or..."

"We get it," Kamal cut in. "Anywhere but your bed."

"Yes," Taiki agreed.

"Would you want to go down those stairs at two in the morning with the house pitch dark?" Naheem asked.

"Just how dark does it get?" Taiki wondered.

"Very dark. You can't see in front of you," Ljerka piped in.

"Oh," was all Taiki said.

Kamal got out the bed and grabbed his shirt. Taiki got a peek at his upper body. Damn, she thought. But she moaned outwardly.

"Everything okay, now, T?" Naheem asked.

"Yes, everything is fine," Taiki answered. "You guys can go."

Ljerka and Naheem left to get dressed. That left Taiki and Kamal alone. He was getting to leave when Taiki stopped him.

"I'm sorry about that," Taiki apologized. "I'm not used to men in the bed without them saying or doing anything the night before."

"Oh okay," was Kamal said leaving.

He walked past Taiki to the door when she grabs his arm. She turns towards him and goes on her tippy toes then kisses him.

"What was that for?" Kamal wondered. "Not that I'm complaining."

"Curiosity," Taiki answered. "Just curiosity." Letting him go.

"That was some curiosity," he said. "Let me satisfy my curiosity."

He leaned down and kissed her lips as he wrapped his arms around her. He pulled back. "Damn," Kamal moaned.

"What?" Taiki wondered.

"Damn," he moaned again.

He kissed her again. He broke off the kiss long enough to close the door behind him. He walked her to the bed and undressed her. He walked her to the bed and laid her down. He lays next to her and continues to kiss her while her runs his hand up and down her body.

She opens her legs for him as he slides two fingers inside her. She stoked his cock as he did so. She the felt him lay between her thighs as he slides himself inside her. She feels him moves in and out of her. She met him stroke for stroke.

"Aahh," they moan together.

Kamal kissed down her neck to her breasts and then sucked on her nipples. He feels her hands in his hair. "Damn!" he heard her moan as he rolls over still inside her. He lay on his back with Taiki on top.

Taiki rides him fast and hard. She lays her hands on his chest to push him against the mattress. "Shit!" she hears him moan. She leans down and kisses his neck down to his chest. She feels his nipples harden. "Aahh," she then hears him moan.

"I guess they're getting on well," Ljerka commented walking hand and hand with Naheem down to the kitchen.

"And it's not even the Sin Festival," Naheem added raising their intertwined hands up and kiss her hand before putting them down.

"Wait, isn't the Sin Festival this weekend?" she asked.

"Yes," he answered. "It's tonight actually." Going down the stairs a head of her.

"Tonight? Time goes fast."

"Not really." He laughed. "Your days must be running together."

Chuckling. "Must be. I don't know if I like it."

Back upstairs, Kamal and Taiki lay in each other arms. He was still inside her.

"Mmm," Taiki moans. "Damn," she then moans.

"Yes," Kamal moans kissing her lips.

Taiki moves off Kamal and gets up and heads towards the bathroom. She tries the door and it was locked. "Kamal, could you...?" she requested. He got and unlocked the door.

"Where are you going?" Kamal asked.

"Shower then getting something to eat," she answered.

"I'll meet you downstairs," he said.

"Why?"

"If I have shared a shower with you now, I won't have enough energy for tonight,"

"What's tonight?"

"The Sin Festival. Festival of Sex."

"Oh, Ljerka told me about that."

"What she tells you?"

"Just the basics. What you do. What happens, etc."

"Wait until you experience it. You'll love it. Lots and lots of sex. The atmosphere will be thick with sex."

"Mmm, damn! I just might." Opening the door and walking out.

Following her part ways. "I'll meet you down there." Then kissed her.

Kissing him back. "All right."

They parted their separate ways. Taiki to the bathroom to shower and Kamal downstairs.

Chapter 8

Ljerka, Kamal, Taiki and Naheem sat eating breakfast in the small dinning room. Seija and Juliano came in and joined them. Seija still was angry that they were there. They shouldn't be here, she thought.

Later that night, before moonrise, Ljerka met her parents. Dovie and Marty Hegarty sat on the couch closest to Ljerka's. Taiki and Naheem sat on either side of Ljerka holding her hand for support.

"Ljerka, nice to meet you," Dovie Hegarty said.

"Nice to meet you, too, Mrs. Hegarty," Ljerka said back.

Marty Hegarty didn't say anything, just stared. He kept starring until his wife elbowed him in the side to get his attention. "Sorry, what did you say?" he asked. "I can't help be stare."

"That's okay," Ljerka said.

"We never though we'd see you again," Dovie said.

"After what happened..." Marty started to say but was cut off by his wife elbowing him in the side.

"What do you mean after what happened to me?" demanded Ljerka.

Mr. and Mrs. Hegarty held hands and started the story.

"When you and Eve were five months old, you both became sick. We thought both of you would make it. Especially you..." Marty explained.

"Why not me?" Ljerka asked.

"You had really bad heart problems when you were born due to you being a premature," said Dovie.

"I was premature?" the younger woman said in wonder.

"Yes, you were about 3.4 lbs. You were smaller than Eve. We didn't think you'd make it." The older woman said.

"Oh wow, 3.4 lbs. My foster parents didn't tell me that."

"About that, they kidnapped from the hospital when you were sick," Marty said.

"I was, what?!" Ljerka exclaimed.

"You were kidnapped from the Goldenleaf NICU. The police couldn't find you, but we never stopped looking. I always hoped you find your way back to us," Dovie explained.

"Who took me?" Ljerka demanded squeezing both Naheem and Taiki's hands for support waiting for the answer.

"We don't know," Marty answered.

"We never were able to find out," Dovie added. "They said it could have been one of the nurses because they told us you died, and they wouldn't let us see you."

"How is that possible? How could do...?" letting Taiki and Naheem's hands go to stand and pace the room.

Dovie got up to stop Ljerka but she just jerked away. That when Marty got up and stopped her. They hugged her as Ljerka cried. Naheem and Taiki left the room to give them privacy. When Ljerka was all cried out, she hugged them back.

"This is going to be a big problem now that she found her parents," Seija said. "What are we going to do about it?"

"I don't know," the other woman said. "This was your idea to get rid of her."

"This was both our idea, Enis," she countered.

"True but you have more at stake then I do, Seija."

Juliano walked up to them. He didn't like what he just overheard. "What do you have at stake, Seija?"

"Nothing, Juliano," Seija lied to her husband.

"Are you in trouble, bae?" he then asked.

"No, hun," she continued to lie.

In the back of Juliano's mind, he knew his wife was lying to him but didn't understand why. He just let it go.

It was almost moonrise, time for the Sin Festival. Dovie and Marty Hegarty promised Ljerka that they would call once she left town. She promised to call and visit while she was in town. Ljerka was happy she finally met her parents. Taiki was happy, too.

Ljerka and Taiki was in Ljerka's room getting ready for the Sin Festival. She helped Taiki pick out a thin enough robe to go downstairs in. Once they found one, it was time to go downstairs.

They made it downstairs right when the clock chimed. Naheem and Kamal met them at the bottom of the stairs. They gently grabbed their hands and walked to a private area of the room. They disrobed as they kissed each other. They women moaned as the men then kissed their necks to the breasts and nipples. They held their heads as they did so.

Taiki pushed Kamal away and kissed down his body to suck on his cock.

"Fuck!" Kamal moaned moving against Taiki's mouth.

Once he was hard, he pulled away as she stood up. Kamal laid Taiki down and laid between her thighs. He then slid down and parted her as he sucked on her clit and fingered her pussy.

"Aahh...Shiiitt!" Taiki moans a loud as she climaxes.

Kamal kiss up her body to her lips. She tastes herself on his lips. He enters her wet moist pussy. They both together. They meet each other stroke for stroke. They moan as they continue to kiss.

"Can't believe they...brought a outside here," Seija scoffed. "The nerve," she said angerly.

"Why do you care?" Juliano paused briefly on top of her.

"That's my brother."

"You weren't saying that when you were eating the woman's cooking."

"A girl got to eat and so does... her husband."

"True," he agreed as he resumed pumping into her. "True."

"Naheem..." Ljerka moaned riding him.

"Hmmm" Naheem moaned holding her hips.

"Your brother..." she started.

"You really want to... talk about him... now," he moaned.

"Yes, Mmm," her pussy squeezing around him.

"Aahh...Fine. Fine."

"Your brother and my friend are getting on pretty well," Moving on him.

"Mmm...yea, you doubted they would," moving him hips.

"Kind of...yes, I did."

Naheem stopped moving and stopped her. "Why?"

"I don't know but now," Ljerka said.

"But now, what?" he asked.

"But now T, she picky and..." she answered.

"I get it. I get it." Nodding then lifted his hips up. "Enough talking."

"Are you saying I talk to much?"

"Yes," then he pulled her down to kiss her passionately.

They moans together as he moves under her. She leans back and he takes her breasts and nipples in his mouth. She held his head to her as she bites her bottom lip.

Chapter 9

The next day, Taiki cooked once again, this time it was breakfast. Ljerka, Naheem, Kamal, Taiki, Seija, and Juliano sat on the back patio table. They chatted. Naheem invited Ljerka's parents over but they declined. Dovie decided on dinner at their place. Ljerka agreed and asked to bring Taiki. Marty said it was okay.

Some hours later, Ljerka and Taiki was at the Hegarty's place. Dovie showed Ljerka and Taiki baby pictures of Eve and her but mostly of Eve. That was all she had. Ljerka took out her pictures, from when she was a child, that she brought with her.

"Oh my...," Dovie said in shock. "Marty, come here a second," she called looking at Ljerka's pictures.

"Okay," Marty said coming in the living room a few minutes later. "What's up?!"

"Look at this," she said showing him the pictures.

"Oh my go..." he exclaimed. "She... she... she..."

"I know. I know. Crazy, huh?"

"Yes."

"What? What?" Ljerka demanded.

"We know who took you," Dovie answered.

"Who took me?" Ljerka said.

"A nurse named Devan Pittman. She must go by Devan Tarrant, now," Dovie explained.

"I heard that name before. She was wanted to have a child but couldn't," Ljerka recalled. "No wonder we moved around so much."

"How many times did you move?" Marty wondered.

"About six or seven times before we settled into Eastborne Falls," Ljerka said.

"Eastborne Falls?" Dovie asked. "We used to visit there all the time for work. You were so close but so far."

"Exactly," Ljerka agreed.

When it was time to leave, Ljerka got Dovie and Marty's numbers but Ljerka and Taiki left. Ljerka drove them to Naheem's house. They got out and went inside. No one was around but them so they went upstairs. They went in their rooms. They laid on their bed and went to sleep.

About forty minutes later, Naheem and Kamal went to Ljerka and Taiki's rooms. They got into bed and snuggled with them. The women snuggled closer to them in their sleep.

Downstairs, Seija and Enis were talking.

"Something has to be done with them," Enis sneered.

"What am I supposed to do?" Seija demanded.

"They're your brothers," Enis said. "Do something about it? They're getting too close to them."

"I know. I know."

"What are you going to do about then?"

"I don't know yet but I'll think of something. I think Jules is getting suspicious."

"He getting suspicious of what?"

"Of us not liking Ljerka and Taiki."

"So, we don't. Why hide it?"

"Because I don't want conflict in my family. With my brothers."

"Can't really prevent that because of what happened."

"Shhh. Quiet or everyone will hear."

"So, what?"

"So, what? So, what! Kamal and Naheem are my brothers, damn it!"

"So fucking what?" Enis said slowly.

"Well, fuck you them!" Seija cursed at her then stormed off.

Ljerka woke up to feet stomping up the stairs. "Umm," she groaned.

"Seija's mad at someone," Naheem commented without opening his eyes.

"What's that?" she asked turning toward him.

"My sister only stomps up the stairs when she's mad at someone," he explained.

"Oh. Well, she needs to stop being mad because it just woke me up."

"I'll be sure to tell her."

Ljerka sent him a look.

"Okay, sorry," Naheem apologized.

All she did was nodded. "What time is it?"

"I don't know. Why?" he asked.

"Because I need..."

"Me," kissing her neck.

"No!"

"No?" fingering her through her clothes.

"I mean no, not right now."

"Okay," pulling away. "What do you mean?"

"I'm... I need to call Dovie and Marty."

"For what?"

"They needed something some paperwork from me."

"Do you have the paperwork with you?"

"Yes, I do in my luggage. I meant to get it out but I fell a sleep."

"What's the paperwork?"

"It's nothing to worry about, Naheem," reassuring him. "Nothing bad."

"I still want to know, Ljerka."

"Fine. They wanted the..." Someone knocked on the door. "Saved by the knock."

"Who is it?" Naheem yelled.

"Jaxon. It's Jaxon," he yelled back. "I need to talk to you...Privately."

Naheem groaned as he got up. "Hold on a minute."

"I'll be in your office. I'll get Kamal. He needs to hear this," Jaxon said.

"I'll get him," his boss said.

Naheem and Ljerka hears Jaxon's foot stepped leaving. He got up. "This isn't over," leaving the room.

In Naheem's office, the men of Naheem's circle was there. Jaxon spoke up.

"We need to do something about your sister, Seija, and Enis," Jaxon said.

"Why?" Naheem and Kamal demanded.

"Because I overheard them plotting against Taiki and Ljerka," he answered.

"Ljerka," Naheem corrected. "Continue."

"Well, they, Seija and Enis, doesn't like Taiki and Ljerka," Jaxon said. "They might do something them."

"How do you know this?" Kamal asked.

"As I said I heard them," he answered.

Juliano didn't looked the least bit shocked.

"Why don't you look surprised, Jules?" Naheem demanded.

"That is because I also overheard them, too, "Juliano said. "I even talked to Seija about it."

"And you didn't come to me about it?" Naheem demanded angrly.

"Sorry but...," Juliano apologized.

"But nothing!" Naheem shouted. "You should have came to me about this."

"Your sister. My wife is my first loyalty." Juliano stated.

"Hmm," was all Naheem said. "I see."

"Will you be doing something about them, then?" Kamal asked his brother.

Naheem sighed looking at Juliano and thought about his sister. *They're harmless*, he thought. "Nothing for now," he said. "But we should keep an eye on them."

The men nodded in agreement. Naheem hoped he wasn't wrong.

Chapter 10

Ljerka and Taiki took Katharina and Levi to the park not far from Underfield Winter House. Underfield Winter House was owned by Kamal, Naheem, and Seija other sibling, brother named Tristan. He was the third oldest out of the boys.

"Thanks, Tristan, for showing us the way to the park," Ljerka thanked him.

"No problem, hun," Tristan said. "Any friend of Naheem is a friend of mine."

The children enjoyed the park as Taiki and Ljerka talked. Katharina came over to them.

"Ljerka?" Katharina said.

Looking over at the little. "Yes?" Ljerka asked.

"Do you like my dad?" the little girl asked.

"Yes, I do," Ljerka answered. "I really do."

"Good," Katharina said. "You remind me of mommy," then ran off.

"Aww, Ljerka," Taiki gushed.

"I know," Ljerka said.

Meanwhile, Kamal and Naheem joined Ljerka and Taiki at the park. They sat at the table next to them. They kissed in greeting.

"They seem to be having fun," Naheem stated looking at his children play.

"Yes, they are," Ljerka said. "I had a talk with Katharina..."

"About what?" he asked.

"About if I liked you and I remind her of Eve," she answered.

"Oh I'm sorry. She..."

"It's fine. I was actually flattered after the shock."

"Oh okay good. I didn't know if..."

"They're fine, Naheem. Eve would have been proud."

Levi and Katharina must have heard their father's voice because they came running to the table they were sitting.

"Daddy!" they yelled as they ran.

"Hey, you little monsters," their father greeted them jokingly. "You being good for Taiki and Ljerka?"

"Yes," Levi said leaping on the table. Katarina nodded in agreement as she leaped on Naheem's lap.

"Good," Naheem said. "Say thank you to Ljerka and Taiki for taking you the park."

"Thank you," Levi and Katharina in unison.

"Now it's time to go," he then said the them. "It's time to eat."

"Aww," they wined.

"We're staying at Uncle Tristan and Marcos's house for dinner," Kamal added.

"Yay," they yelled.

They all walked to Tristan and Marcos' house and were greeted by Tristan on the porch.

"Hey, everyone come in. Come in," Tristan said letting them in. "Marcos, my jellybean, they're here."

"Marvelous. Marvelous," Marcos said looking over his shoulder. "Get them drinks," turning to stove. "Dinner is almost ready."

Ljerka and Taiki drank wine. Naheem and Kamal drank beer. The children drank juice. The women joined Marcos in the kitchen.

"What can I do for you, ladies?" Marcos wondered.

"Just came in to talk to you," Taiki answered.

"What about?" he then asked.

"Just curious about how it is marrying a Lukas," Ljerka said.

"What do you mean?"

"Well, they have high sex drives, myself included, but how..." Ljerka explained.

"Yes , I understand," Marcos said. "Well, I am not like them but I have a high sex drive too. So, it's okay with me."

"Okay," Ljerka and Taiki said nodded.

In the dinning room, Tristan, Naheem and Kamal sat to the table with Katharina and Levi watching television in the family room.

"Seija and Enis are up to something," Naheem said. "Keep an eye out for them."

"Where did you hear this?" Tristan wondered.

"Jaxon overheard them," he said.

"How do you know it was something bad?"

"They were talking about Ljerka and Taiki," Kamal added. "About getting rid of them."

"Seija wouldn't do that. It's Seija for crying out loud."

"Yes, but that's what Jaxon said."

"Fine if you believe that's going to happen to them."

The women helped Marcos bring the food into the dinning room. Naheem told Katharina and Levi to wash their hands and come eat. They came back and sat down as their father and Uncles washed their hands, too. The women also washed theirs, too.

"So, how is the wedding coming along?" Naheem asked.

"It's coming along great," Tristan answered.

"Yes, it's coming along great," Marcos agreed. "It's a great that we have a wedding planner. It makes things so much better."

"That's great," Taiki commented. "My brother and his wife had a wedding planner, too. It worked great for them. Everything went smoothly."

"I hope it does for us also," Tristan said looking at Marcos lovingly. "So, how are you liking Goldenleaf so far?"

"It's great you have everything here," Ljerka said as Taiki nodded in agreement. She didn't mention the Sin Festival that happens every weekend.

"Yes, we do," Naheem agreement. "We go out sometime and really show you two around."

"Sounds great," Taiki said answering for the both.

"I will take some time off to do that," Kamal said. "I'll ever show the you Underfield Autumn House," looking at Taiki sensually.

"I'd like that," Taiki said looking into eyes getting the hint. Ljerka kicked her under the table. "I mean we'd like that," then blushed and looked away.

That night, the sexual tension was so thick one could cut it with a knife. The children went to bed and was sleep before their heads hit the pillow. Which was great because they were all ready undressing each other with their eyes.

Kamal took Taiki to Underfield Autumn House. He was already undressing her before they closed the door. It was the same for Ljerka and Naheem and Tristan and Marcos. It was like a wave a sexual energy hit all of them at once. They all moan at once. None of the knew what was going on or even realized.

A several moments later, they all cry out as they climaxed.

Breathing heavy, they pulled apart. *What the hell was that?* they thought. They kiss each other and go to sleep.

"Wow!" Ljerka said shocked. "That was different." Only thing that Naheem could do is nod in agreement. "Wow."

Naheem finally said, "Oh my damn! Oh, my damn!" rolling over onto his back. "How about a round two when I can breathe?"

"Sure, but I need to eat or drink something."

"There is a mini fridge in the bottom of the night table."

Ljerka leaned over and opened the fridge door. She grabbed two bottles of Powerade and handed one to Naheem. She then grabbed two sandwiches and handed him one.

"Thanks," thanked her.

"So, do you have mini fridges in every room?"

"Just about for Sin Festival visitors. Other than that, not really."

"The Sin Festival must bring in a lot of visitors."

"Yes, it does. The Sin Festival is our most popular attraction for having visitors come in. They stay at one of the four Underfield Houses."

"Oh ok."

Chapter 11

The next day, Ljerka and Naheem joined Tristan and Marcos on their patio having brunch. They didn't mention what happened last night. They talked about Tristan and Marcos' wedding.

"So, we are having an outdoor wedding under big tents, just in case the weather is poor," Marcos said.

"Outdoor weddings are great," Ljerka commented. "I once went to an outdoor wedding and had a great time."

"Hopefully, you and Taiki will be here for ours," Tristan said. "Because you two are invited of course."

"Thank you," Ljerka thanked him. "How many visitors are coming to your wedding?"

"Just immediate family and some friends," Marcos answered. "Not many people in town are excepting of us only during the Sin Festival."

"Why?" she wondered.

"Long story. Long story, hun," Tristan answered. "I'd hate to bore you."

"No, you're fine."

"Okay. Well, before I came, I was always a part of town doing manly jobs and such."

"Go on," she encouraged him to go on.

"I sort of flirted with some of the men, I had sex with during Sin Fest and they didn't like it. Also, they're wives didn't either," Tristan chuckled at the end. Everyone else chuckled, also. Well anyway..."

A woman came out and whispered in Tristan's ear.

"Sorry, excuse me a moment," Tristan said excused himself.

Tristan got up and went back in the house. A few minutes later, he came out and got Marcos. They then both came out and seat down.

"Everything okay?" Naheem asked.

"Yes, we just had call from our adoption specialist. Everything is going on as scheduled," Tristan informed them.

"Aww wow!" his brother said excitedly. "Congratulations!" patting his brother on the back.

"Thanks," Tristan thanked them.

"Thank you," Marcos thanked them.

"Boy or girl?" Ljerka asked.

"Twin sibling: a boy and a girl," Tristan said.

A few minutes later, the four of them all hugged and said goodbye.

Naheem and Ljerka meet up with Kamal and Taiki in town. They walked around town and went into the stores. Taiki was shocked like Ljerka was when she first came into town.

"They really hang those up all the time?" Taiki asked.

"Yes, they do," Kamal answered. "It gets you in the spirit."

"In the spirit to have sex," Ljerka stated. "Whoa."

"You two will get used to it," Naheem said. "Ljeri, you were here for three or four of the Sin Fests."

"Yeah, I remember," she said.

"I thought Climax was bad," Taiki chuckled.

"Climax?!" Kamal said shocked. "You went to Climax?"

"Yes, I did. Ljerka took me," Taiki explained.

"And she didn't participate but her top was undone," Ljerka added.

"Ljerka!" Taiki scolded. "That didn't happen."

"Did you or did you not have your shirt undone when you came and got me to leave?"

"Okay fine. It was but not in the way you said."

"Hahahahaha, I'm just playing."

"That's not funny, Ljeri," chuckling. "I got you next time."

"Look at them," Seija sneered watching Naheem, Kamal, Ljerka, and Taiki walk into a store.

"Yeah," Enis agreed.

"We have to do something about them in a hurry."

"Yes, we do but what?"

"We'll think of something."

Meanwhile inside the store, Ljerka and Taiki looked around. They found little things to bring back home. Naheem and Kamal huddled talking.

"Well, everything seems to be going well with you and Taiki," Naheem commented.

"Yes, it is," Kamal agreed. "You seem surprised."

"I kind of am. You don't usually click with a woman well. Also, from what Ljerka says about Taiki, she's picky about who she dates and has sex with."

"I usually don't click well with women because..."

Kamal was cut off when Taiki and Ljerka came over and shown him and Naheem what they bought. The women handed the men their shopping bags.

"We should have brought my car," Naheem joked.

"I think that's a good idea," Kamal agreed joked.

The four of them walked out the store onto the street. They walked to the next store. It was the lingerie shop called Goldenleaf Lingerie Boutique. It was a unisex shop. The women went in alone leaving the men to talk to Marty outside. It was owned by Ljerka and Eve's mother, Dovie.

"Hey, girls," Dovie said greeting them.

"Hey," Ljerka greeted her.

"Hi," Taiki greeted her.

"So, what brings you in?"

"We're looking for lingerie for Naheem and Kamal," Ljerka told her.

"Wow, so you two are there now?" Dovie wondered walking them to the bras.

"Kamal keeps ripping my bras and panties," Taiki answered.

"Naheem does, too," Ljerka added. "This is awkward talking to you about all this."

"I know," Dovie said gently. "But I'm used to it. Eve..."

"Yes, I know," Ljerka said understanding.

Dovie handed, Ljerka and Taiki, bras they might like and to see if they can fit them. "How about these? I'll get you two some panties to try on." Then ushered them into the fitting room in the back of the boutique and left again.

Ljerka and Taiki closed their curtains and tried the bras on.

"Wow!" Taiki said shocked.

"I know right," Ljerka agreed with her.

"How did she find out about our sizes?" Taiki asked.

"How are the bras fitting?" Dovie asked outside their fitting rooms. Peeking their heads out. "How...?"

"I am good at my job," the older woman said.

"Very good," Taiki added. Ljerka nodded in agreement.

"Thank you," thanking them. "Here you go try these on. They should match the bras or in similar color and design."

Ljerka and Taiki took the panties handed out to them. They ducked back inside and tried on the panties.

"Damn, she good," Ljerka said to herself.

Naheem and Kamal came into the boutique and waiting in front. Marty decided to show the men's side of the boutique. There was boxers and form fitting underwear to pick from. Also, tee- shirts and wife beaters.

"Marty, when did you open a men's side?" Naheem asked.

"About two months ago," Marty answered. "You don't come to town much."

"I go out of town on business a lot," Kamal countered.

"I am glad you're in town now," Marty said.

"Me too," Kamal agreed.

"When do you leave again?" Naheem asked.

"Two weeks," Kamal answered. "I'll be going to..."

Before Kamal could answer, they were invaded by women. Three in particular, Ljerka, Taiki, and Dovie, walked over to them.

"I thought you guy were going to stay outside," Ljerka said.

"Marty wanted to show us the new the men's area," Naheem explained.

"Oh wow," she said. "It looks nice. You should see the lingerie we picked out."

"Ljerka!" Taiki scolded. "I thought we were going to surprise them."

"I was too excited to keep it to myself, sorry," Ljerka apologizes.

"Yeah right," Taiki said.

The four of them went up to the register and cashed out. They then left out the boutique. They went back to Naheem's house. They went to Ljerka and Taiki's rooms and Naheem and Kamal followed. The women changed into the bras and panties, they bought, for the men then men changed into their boxers, they bought.

"Damn!" they said to each other.

"Those are gorgeous," Kamal and Naheem commented.

The women did a mock curtsy and went over to kiss them.

That night, the two women went to Tristan and Marcos' house to visit with Marcos. Marcos made cocktails for them. They lounged by the pool as the talked.

"So, how is the fostering going?" Taiki wondered.

"It's going great," Marcos answered. "We should be getting the two children next week."

"That's awesome," Ljerka excited for them. "I'm so happy for you."

"Me too. "Taiki piped up.

"Thank you, ladies," Marcos thanked him. "So, how long are you two are going to be in Goldenleaf?"

"Well, we are going to be leaving in about a month maybe earlier because of work," Taiki answered.

"Why don't you work here?" he wondered.

"Can't," Ljerka said. "We didn't bring any work with us."

"How do your coworker and employees get a hold of you two?"

"Email and conference calls," Taiki answered. "So far, they didn't need any help, which is good. Knock on wood."

Marcos chuckled sipping his cocktail. "That's good."

"Yeah," Taiki agreed taking a sip.

They sipped their cocktails and continues to talk. Marcos gets up to fill up their glasses.

"Why a month?" Ljerka asked.

"So, you can make plans to come back," Taiki explained. "We need to get back and see our clients."

"They haven't called, have they?"

"No, but you never know."

"True." Taking another sip of her drink.

"Yeah." Also taking a sip, also.

Marcos came back out with the pitcher of cocktails. He was upset. Ljerka and Taiki immediately and went to him.

"What's wrong?" the women asked in unison as Ljerka took the pitcher away then it on the table.

"Oh, it's nothing," Marcos said. "Just was told there was a hick up with our adoption."

"Oh no," the women just said.

"What is the hick up?" Ljerka asked.

"They told me that we need a reference that not family or the family I'm marring into," he told them. "What are Tristan and I going to do?" he cried.

"We'll give you the reference if you want, right Ljeri," Taiki volunteered.

"Right, we will," Ljerka agreed.

Hugging them both, "Oh, thank you. Thank you," he thanked them. "I can't to tell Tristan." Then ran into the house for the phone.

"We're giving them a reference...we don't even know them," Ljerka said.

"True but I think we're going to be around them for a while," Taiki said.

"Yes, I know but..."

Before she could finish, Marcos came back out and plopped down in the chair. "Whoa! Yes!" he sighed.

"I understand where you are coming from," Taiki commented.

"Yes," Marcos sighed again.

Chapter 12

Naheem, Kamal, and Tristan sat sipping beers, talking. Basically, having a brother's night. They talked about the adoption and the phone calls Tristan just got. Kamal and Naheem was shocked that Taiki and Ljerka was going to help Marcos and Tristan with references.

"They are so nice to do for that for us," Tristan said in awe.

"Yes, they are," Naheem agreed.

"Yes, they are," Kamal also agreed.

"I can't still believe that they decided to do it, even though, they don't know us well," Tristan continued in awe.

Tristan's brothers nodded in agreement. They walked to Naheem's study as they lit up cigars. He opened the door then they all went inside. Kamal plopped down on the couch. Tristan leaned against the desk. Naheem sat in his office chair.

"'Heem, you need to change this office," Tristan said.

"Why?" Naheem demanded. "I like it."

"It's dark. You need to turn on the light during the daytime," the youngest brother explained.

"Here we go," the middle brother mocks groaned.

The eldest brother mocks groaned, also. "Not again."

"Listen to me. I have better taste than you."

"That may be true, TL., but I like it the way it is."

"Fine, but if you change your mind..."

"And I won't."

"If you change your mind..." he repeated. "... you know my number, cell and all."

"Yes, I do."

Taiki and Ljerka stayed at Tristan and Marcos' guest rooms because they were too drunk to drive across town to Naheem's house. Tristan left Naheem's house at midnight to go home. He made it there at around twelve thirty.

Naheem and Kamal was glad Taiki and Ljerka made it home the next morning. They were hung over but all around all right. They took something the pain and laid back down.

Ljerka and Taiki woke up at about five minutes to two in the afternoon. They showered and went to get something to eat. They walked in the kitchen and saw Kamal cooking brunch. Naheem handed them both juice and piece of toast. They ate the toast as they sat at the counter.

"So, what's for lunch?" Taiki asked.

"It smells good," Ljerka commented.

"Thank you, ladies," Kamal thanked them. "Are you up for a bite?"

"I think so," Taiki answered. "What about you, Ljerka?"

"Yea, I feel much better," Ljerka answered.

"All right," he said as he dished up plates for them.

Kamal handed them to Naheem to hand to them. As they ate, their stomach settled. They ate in peace. Levi and Katharina came in.

"Can we have some?" Levi and Katharina asked.

"Can you say Hello to everyone first?" Naheem countered.

"Hello," the children greeted them.

"Now, can we eat?" Katharina asked in such a serious face that Ljerka, Naheem, Kamal, and Taiki laughed.

"Rina!" her father scolded her laughing.

"Sorry but I'm hungry," Katharina apologized.

"Me too," Levi added adding himself in.

"Go head but be careful," Naheem said.

They dished themselves up plates and sat at the table with the older people.

"Levi, Rina, Uncle TL. is adoption two children about your guys ages," their father told them.

"When?" Levi asked.

"In about a week or so," Naheem told them.

"What's their names?" Katharina then asked.

"We don't know yet," Kamal said.

"Okay," Levi and Rina said as they finished up eating then got up to leave.

"Plates... in the rinsed off and in the dishwasher," Ljerka said in a motherly tone.

They did as they were told. Taiki and Kamal looked at weird where as Naheem just gave her a wink. The children then left the kitchen.

"What was that all about?" Taiki demanded.

"Sorry but..." Ljerka answered.

"You were fine," Naheem said. "She was fine. They need to learn to put the dishes in the dishwasher."

"True but she went all mother like and all," Kamal commented.

"Yeah," Taiki agreed.

Later that night, the Sin Festival started. Everyone was in the sexual groove when a big boom sounded. The lights went out and the black light came on. No one stopped what they were doing but Kamal, Taiki, Ljerka, and Naheem.

"What happened to the lights?" Taiki asked.

"What was that noise?" Ljerka then asked.

"I think power was knocked," Kamal answered.

"It does that sometimes," Naheem added kissing her neck. "Don't you like the lights?" then started fingering her.

"Yes," she moans. "I like it... Aahhh!"

Ljerka grabbed gently to turn Naheem's head and kissed him. She then reached down, gripped his cock, and stroked his cock as she grinds against his hand.

The next day, Ljerka and Naheem sat in the smaller living room with Kamal and Taiki. They talked and joked around until Taiki got a call. She walked out the living room and went to her bedroom for privacy.

"Hello?" Taiki answered the phone.

"Ms. Zampino, the invoice you sent needs work," the man said.

"What is wrong with it?" she asked pulling her laptop out of her travel bag.

Taiki turned it on and pulled up the invoice in question.

"All right," she said. "I'm looking at it. I see nothing wrong."

"The Partners are complaining about the way you worded it," he explained. "Plus, you need to explain your pitch in person."

"In person?!" she yelled. "Why can't I just face time call?"

"Why can't you come in?" he countered.

"I am out of town but will be back in three weeks."

"Oh, I see."

"I'll resend the invoice and present it in about a week." A knock came at her bedroom door. "I have to go. I will get those done. Have a nice day, goodbye."

Taiki hung up as someone knock her door again.

"Come in," she said.

The door opened and Ljerka peeked her head in.

"Is everything okay?" Ljerka asked.

"No," Taiki said. "The Partners wants a new invoice and presentation," she explained.

"When are they due?" Ljerka asked in her business voice.

"I asked for a week."

"That's good thing, right?"

"Sort of."

"Why sort of?"

"Because everything I need is at the house."

"Shit!"

"I know."

"We all could take a drive to Eastbourne Falls. I can show Naheem and Kamal around."

"Sounds good but doesn't Naheem and Kamal have jobs to run?"

"I think they do but we can see if they can take a break."

"Yeah, we could ask," getting up to leave with Ljerka.

Both Ljerka and Taiki went down the stairs and joined Kamal and Naheem in the living room again. They sit down.

"Everything, okay?" Kamal asked. "I heard yelling."

"It's okay," Taiki answered. "Just that something with work."

"Anything we could help with?" Naheem asked.

"Actually... you can. We need to go back home so, T can send some papers off and do a presentation," Ljerka explained.

"Sounds good but for how long?" Kamal wondered.

"Just a couple of days or so," Taiki answered. "Why?"

"I have to go in a week for a business trip," Kamal said.

"Oh okay," Taiki just said.

"Yeah, I'll be back the week or two after that."

"All right. We can be together now."

Kamal wasn't satisfied with Taiki answer, but he didn't say so.

Chapter 13

Two or three days later, Naheem, Ljerka, Kamal, and Taiki were in Ljerka and Taiki's apartment sitting, on the couch and love seat, watching movies. Ljerka started to yawn then Naheem. They got up walked back to Ljerka's bedroom.

"Is everything okay with T?" Naheem wondered.

"Not why?" Ljerka countered.

"She's acting strange toward Kamal," he commented.

"She's fine," she reassured him. "Just concerned with work. The Partners aren't happy with her right now and she stressed."

"Oh."

"Yeah."

In the living room, Kamal and Taiki snuggled on the couch finishing the movie they started.

"Everything okay?" Kamal wondered.

"Just worried about the presentation and invoice I need to send in," Taiki explained.

"Do you need help with it?" he asked. "Great with both."

"No, I can't ask of that of you," she said. "But how good?"

"Very good."

"How writing sale pitches to Partners of Art and Lands?"

"I thought you owned Partners of Art and Lands."

"I do but I still answer to someone. It happens to be a company we are trying to buy and flip. They don't like the presentation to one of my employees presented."

"Oh okay, I see. What's the company called?"

"The Orange Tile and Style."

"That's one of my beginner companies."

"Really so I can just..."

In his business voice. "Just because we're sleeping together doesn't mean I'm giving you my company."

"Well shit, I didn't think you would ask... What kind of businesswoman do think, I am?!"

"How should I know?!"

"I look like someone that would do that?"

"I never did work with you work wise."

"I'm starting the invoice and presentation."

Watching her getting up leave. "Taiki, wait. Don't be mad, please. I didn't know."

Taiki continues to leave and went to her room. She then slams the door.

"Shit!" Kamal cursed.

Naheem came out of Ljerka's room. He walked back to the living room. "What the hell happened now?" he demanded.

"She is the one who's trying to buy my company, Heem," Kamal explained.

"What?!"

"Yeah, she and her company called Partners of Art and Lands."

"Damn bro. Damn."

"So, we were fighting over that."

"This time."

"Yeah, this time. She is working on her pitch now."

"Right now, at almost eleven at night."

"Yes, at almost eleven at night." Confirming what his brother said.

"She must be really mad."

"You think?!"

"You don't have to be sarcastic. Anyway, why don't you talk to her because you're going to have to work this out?"

"True."

"Also, because you two fighting is killing my vibe with Ljerka."

"Do you always have to think with your cock, bro?"

"Oh, and two, bro, you are on your own." Then Naheem walked back into Ljerka's room and closed the door behind him.

"Shit!" Kamal cursed again.

Meanwhile in Taiki's room, she was still working on her pitch and presentation to present it to Kamal in the morning when a knock at the door sounded.

"What?!" she yelled.

"It's Ljerka!" Ljerka yelled.

"Come in!"

Ljerka opened the door and came in. She watched her friend pouring over spread sheets, files, and other things. "T, do you think you should work on that when you have company?"

"What company? Mr. Lukas is a potential client," Taiki said.

"Damn, T! You know very well that Kamal likes you and want to be with you."

Taiki doesn't say anything just continues working. She didn't stop until Ljerka left and closed the door softly. "Shit!" she cursed then shook her head.

The next day, the tension between Kamal and Taiki was thick as a knife. Neither yelled at each other. Ljerka and Naheem talked as Taiki and Kamal just sat there. By the end of the next day, Ljerka and Naheem was tired of the silence.

"You two are going to listen," Naheem ordered.

Kamal and Taiki looked at the them but said nothing.

"We're tired of this arguing between you two," Naheem continued. "We thought you two were hitting it off."

"We were until..." Taiki starting to argue.

"She didn't let me explain..." Kamal countered argued.

"Don't care what started it," Ljerka cutting them both off. "It's going to stop today. it's the Sin Festival tonight and I don't want your tension to back the mood."

Taiki and Kamal looked at each other then looked away. They got up and went their separate ways. They slam doors behind them.

"That went well," Ljerka said sarcastically.

"Yeah," Naheem agreed sarcastically.

During the time of the Sin Festival, Kamal walked around town. Taiki was still working on her work and hearing her friends fuck. She decided to leave the apartment and go for a walk. She didn't know that she was absentmindedly walking toward Kamal.

Kamal decided to walk back to Ljerka and Taiki's house. He also decided to make amends with Taiki and celebrate Sin Fest. He sees Taiki walking towards him. She wasn't looking to happy, he thought.

"Take it slow, Kamal," he ordered himself.

A few seconds later, Taiki and Kamal stopped in front of each other on the sidewalk two blocks from Ljerka and Taiki's place.

"I want to apologize for making you upset, T," Kamal apologized.

"I'm sorry I got upset with you, but you could have..." Taiki replied.

"Seriously?" he cried. "You... Know what never mind. If you can't take my apology, then..."

"Then, what?" she demanded.

"Then I'll just do this..." He kissed her.

Pulling away. "Why you?!" slapping him and kissed him back.

Chapter 14

Ljerka and Naheem lay in bed cuddling after they climaxed four times. They were work on up the energy for number five. They knew that wasn't going to happen, but they wanted to try.

Thirty minutes later, they got up and looked to see where Taiki and Kamal went. They then heard noises from the garage apartment. They went back to the house.

"I guess they made up," Ljerka said.

"Good. Good," Naheem replied.

The next day, Ljerka and Naheem lay in each other's arms. Ljerka woke first and went in the bathroom to shower. She gets inside and starts to bathe herself. As the water ran, Naheem woke up and reach for her but, her side was empty. He gets up and went to the bathroom. As he relieves himself, he watched through her the curtain.

As he watched, Naheem grew hard again. "Shit!" he cursed.

In the shower, Ljerka screamed because she thought she was alone. "Naheem?"

"Yeah?" he answered.

"What are you doing in here?" she demanded.

"I needed to pee so I'm going to pee."

"Couldn't you wait?"

"No, when you have to go, you got to go."

"True but..."

"Do you really want to talk about this?"

"What do you mean?"

Naheem pulls back the shower curtain to flash Ljerka.

"Oh..." Ljerka said looking at his face to his cock. "Damn!"

"Yeah, well," Naheem said then got in the shower and pulled the curtain closed.

They started to kiss and feeling on each other's bodies. He then started to kiss on her neck and shoulders. He then turned she away from him and entered her pussy from behind. She was slick and wet for him.

"Aahh," they moan together. "Mm mm!"

A knock sounded on the front door but ignored it. The phone then rang, they ignored that too.

Naheem pumped into Ljerka as he held onto her hips. He then reaches to turn off the water because he almost drowning. He continues to pump hard and fast into her. He reaches around and plays with her clit.

Ljerka moans long and loud as she moves against his finger. "Oh my god! Oh my god! "I'm coming! I'm coming!"

"Shit! Shit!" he moans as he climaxes and empty himself into her.

Ljerka and Naheem get out the shower and go back to the bedroom. They both get dress and head downstairs. Kamal and Taiki was already down there when they got there. They were all lovey dovey.

"I guess you two really made up," Ljerka commented.

All Taiki did was nodded and Kamal kissed her neck making her giggle.

"We have a surprise for you two," Taiki said.

"What is it?" Ljerka asked. "I love surprises."

Kamal grabbed something from off the floor. "Tada!"

It was a toy. Not any toy but an adult toy.

"Hahaha!" Ljerka laughed. "What's that for?"

"You know," Kamal wiggled his eyebrows.

"Seriously!" Naheem chuckling.

The doorbell sounded.

Ljerka went to answer the door. When she looked through the peephole, it was Omar on the other side. She rushed and opened door.

"What are you doing here?" she demanded.

"I came to see you, baby," Omar said as he was about to kiss her.

Pulling up her hand to stop him. "I'm busy, Omar."

"Come on. Can I come in?"

"No, I said I'm busy, Omar."

Naheem walked up behind walked up behind her. "Everything okay here?"

"Shit!" Ljerka cursed. "Naheem, Omar. Omar, Naheem."

"Nice to me you," the men said to each other.

"I meet Omar at Climax," she informed him.

"Oh, that Omar," Naheem said. "Thanks for holding down the fort but I got it from here." Then closed the door in Omar's face.

"Damnit, Heem!" Ljerka cursed at him.

"What?!" he demanded.

"I can't believe you did that!" she yelled at him.

"I don't see the problem."

"The problem is..." walking back in the kitchen.

As they made it to the kitchen, Taiki asks. "Are you two arguing now?"

"Yes," Ljerka answered.

"No," Naheem countered.

"Which one is it?" Kamal asked.

"Omar was at the door..." Ljerka said.

"And I told him I can handle things from here..." Naheem said.

"Then he slammed the door in his face," she said.

"I don't see the problem," Taiki and Kamal commented.

"Wait, you two don't?" Ljerka demanded.

"You're upset over another man," Taiki said.

"Well no but..." Ljerka started to say.

"Well what?" Kamal asked.

"Shit!" Ljerka cursed. "You're making sound crazy."

"Because you're sounding crazy," Naheem said.

Ljerka punched Naheem in the arm then left the room.

"Damnit!" Naheem cursed rubbing his arm leaving after her.

In Ljerka's room, she threw a pillow at the wall. She then picked up another and screamed into it. A knock sounded at her bedroom door.

"What?" Ljerka yelled.

"Ljeri, it's Naheem," Naheem yelled back.

"Go away!" she ordered.

"No, we need to talk," he said.

"Go away! I don't want to talk to you!"

"Well, I want to talk to you," trying the doorknob.

The door wasn't locked so he opened it and went inside. He stood to block the doorway after he closed the door.

"Don't even think about," Naheem said as she was going to throw something at him.

"What do you want?" Ljerka demanded plopping down on her bed.

"I want to talk as I said," he repeated. "Also, ouch. That's some punch."

"Will you leave?" she asks. "And sorry."

"What was that?"

"I said I'm sorry I did that."

"Are you? Are you, Naheem, because it seemed like you liked do it?"

"I kind of liked doing it, I got to admit, but..."

"But nothing!"

"Alright! I was wrong. Can we move past this?"

Ljerka hesitated then nodded. She felt foolish.

"Okay, then ready to eat?" Naheem asked.

She nodded again giving in.

"Alright then. So, are we going to make up or what?" he asked.

"Okay, but I'm still upset," she replied.

"Fine. I'm okay with it," as he pulled her into his arms.

"Okay, then," then began kissing him.

They were kissing when a knock sounded at Ljerka's bedroom door.

"What?!" Naheem yelled as Ljerka kissed on his neck.

"Just seeing if everything is alright," Kamal said.

"Everything's fine. Go away!" his younger brother ordered feeling Ljerka stroke his cock.

"Sorry because..." the older brother said.

"Go away, Heem!" entering her wet pussy.

Kamal walked away and went back to living room. Taiki was cleaning the dishes as Kamal walked in. Damn, he thought as he stared at her.

Taiki looked over at him. "Are you just going to stare or are you going to help?" throwing a dish towel.

Kamal caught the towel as he walked over to sink next to her. He started to dry the dishes and put them away.

"So, how are they?" Taiki asked.

"Everything's fine with them," Kamal answered. "They're making up."

"Good. Good," she replied.

Chapter 15

Later that night, the four of them went out to eat. No one wanted to cook so, they decided to go out. As they sat waiting for their food, they sipped their beers and cocktails. Kamal and Naheem sipped their beers as they watched Ljerka and Taiki talk. They were talking about clothes and work. Mentally, the men were thinking that they're were fucked but in a good way.

Their food came and they began eating. The women started playing footsy with men as they tried to eat. The men kept making choked sounds with their food as they ate. The women would look very concerned but they had a playfulness in their eyes.

On the way home, the men, this time, did the playing. With their clits as they drove. The women moan as they reach over to stroke the men cocks. They were barely in park before they started getting out the car and running into the house. They practically ran to Ljerka and Taiki's bedrooms, shedding clothes along the way. They slam the door behind them.

"Aaahh," they moaned as the men entered the women.

Ljerka and Taiki matches Naheem and Kamal's pace. They moved fast and hard. "Damn!" the men groaned.

"Mmmmmm," the women moaned.

"Aahhh...shiiit!" the four of them moaned as they climaxed.

The four of them laid in each other arms as they fell asleep.

The next day, Taiki, Kamal, Naheem, and Ljerka drove back to Goldenleaf. The women drive them down. Once they were in town, they drive to Underfield Spring House. They went into the house and went to the bedrooms to unpacked. Ljerka and Taiki left the house and went to Dovie's Boutique.

Dovie greeted them at the door. "Hey, girls. Didn't know you were back."

"We just got back today," Ljerka said giving her a hug.

"I missed you girls," the older woman said.

"We were only gone a week," Taiki commented.

"What brings you here?" Dovie wondered.

"We need more bras and panties. Maybe some nighties," Ljerka answered.

Ljerka's phone rings. "Excuse me for a minute." then walked outside.

She answers her phone. "Hello?"

"Ljerka," the man said.

"Slaven? What you want?" she demanded.

"I need to see you," Slaven said.

"If you need money, it's a no."

"Damnit, Ljerka, why not?" he demanded. "I really need it."

"No and I'm not home, Slay."

"Where are you?"

"None of your business."

"Ljeri..."

"No. Goodbye, Slaven," then she hung up the phone and turned it off.

As she walked inside, Ljerka placed her phone back in her purse. She walked over to Dovie and Taiki. "What did I miss?"

"Nothing," Taiki said. "Is everything okay on your side?"

"Yeah," Ljerka lying. Then said, "Slaven."

"Oh okay," her friend said.

"Who is Slaven?" Dovie wondered.

"Her brother," Taiki answered. "Well foster brother now."

"Right."

"Right."

"What's up with him?" Dovie wondered.

"He wanted money as per-usual," Ljerka explained.

"For what?"

"Drugs more than likely."

"Oh okay."

"Yeah."

Dovie showed Ljerka and Taiki the bras, panties, and nighties. The younger women ate dinner with Dovie and Marty at their house. They listened to old stories about Eve when she was little. Ljerka relayed stories about her childhood.

"Oh my god, really," Dovie shocked.

"Really," Ljerka said.

"Oh wow," the older woman said. "You really did that."

"Yeah and Devan had a fit."

"She did. I couldn't sit for a week."

"Good." the older woman chuckled.

"Not funny," Ljerka said. "And was grounded for two."

"Only two?"

"Yeah, she couldn't go for out to a concert, we wanted to go to," Taiki added.

"What concert?" Dovie asked.

"Don't remember," Ljerka answered.

A few hours later, Ljerka and Taiki drove back to Naheem's house. On their way there, Ljerka's car started acting weird. She tried to slow down and couldn't. She then tried to brake and couldn't do that either.

"What's wrong with the car?" Taiki demanded.

"I don't know..." Ljerka said. "Something is wrong with the brakes. I can't stop."

Taiki got her phone out.

"Who are you calling?" Ljerka demanded scared.

"Kamal," Taiki said scared shaking. "He could possible help us."

"All right but have him bring Naheem."

Kamal got the phone and rushed out. He rushed to Naheem's house and demanded to see Naheem. "He's busy, Kamal," Jaxon said.

"Tell him it's Ljerka and Taiki," Kamal said.

Jaxon nodded then rushed off. A few minutes later, Naheem rushed down the hall grabbing him keys.

"Are they okay?" Naheem demanded. "What happened?"

"Ljerka's brakes were cut and she can't stop," Kamal informed his brother.

"Where are they now?"

"Driving from the Haggerty's. Let's go."

Kamal and Naheem rushed to Kamal's truck when they heard Ljerka's car coming up the drive. They were screaming as they flew by. The men ran after the car. The women, the men noticed, were heading to the pond in the backyard.

"Open the car door and jump!" Kamal yelled into the phone.

"Are you crazy?" Taiki yelled back.

"No! Just do it!" he ordered. "Jump!"

"Look, let's jump," Taiki yelled.

"On the count of three," Ljerka yelled.

"One... Two... Three..." they counted then opened the car door and jump out.

They tucked and rolled. Only hurting their legs and arms. They look back in time watch Ljerka's car go into the pond.

"Shit!" Ljerka cursed. "My car!"

"It can be fitted or you can get another," Kamal said.

Ljerka and Taiki nodded as they were helped up.

"I want to know who tried to kill them and now!" Naheem ordered slamming his fists onto his desk.

"Heem, you need to calm down," Kamal said.

"How can you be so calm?! Taiki was in the car, too."

"I know but you can't..."

"Can't what?! Be angry?"

"I'm surprised you aren't.

"I am angry. I'll deal with the person or people who did accordingly."

"Want to help?"

"Yeah, might need it."

"Good."

Chapter 16

In Underfield Spring House, Ljerka and Taiki lay on the couch and love seat trying to calm down. They were still shaking. Jaxon brought them water to drink. They were, also, brought food but refused it.

"I think I'm going to be sick," Ljerka said.

"Me too," Taiki agreed.

Jaxon and Maxim ran grabbed two waste baskets and handed them to the girls.

Tristan and Marcos ran into house to the living room, where Ljerka and Taiki was. The two men looked concerned as they stood in front of them.

"Everything going to be alright," Kamal said. "They're going to be alright."

"How can you be so calm?" Marcos asked Kamal.

"I wish you guys would stop asking me that!" Kamal said. "And someone has to."

"Meeting now," Naheem ordered. "My office."

"I'll stay with the girls," Marcos said.

"Thanks, baby," Tristan thanked him by giving him a smooch.

In Naheem's office, Naheem paced the office then raked the items on desk onto the floor. "Damn it!" he cursed.

"There isn't anything we can do, now," Kamal said. "You don't think I'm angry, too."

"Calm down," Tristan ordered. "Nothing could be done to prevent..."

"Stop telling me to calm down!" Naheem yelled. "Yes, we could have prevented what happened." calming down some. "I just don't want what happened to Eve to happen to Ljerka."

"We know that but..." Tristan started to say.

"But nothing," the middle brother said. "If anything ever happened to Ljerka, I'd... I just can't."

The other two brothers nodded.

In the hallway outside the door, Seija and Enis overheard everything. They looked at each other then nodded. They walk away. Not talking until they got to Sepia's wing of her house.

"What should we do?" Enis demanded.

"The same plan we had from the beginning: to get Naheem or Kamal to be with you," Seija answered. "We can't have those two bitches in the way.

"Right, but neither of them like me like that."

"So what, they will."

"What's in it for you?"

"Nothing. Just the pleasure of getting rid of the Haggerty's children."

"What about your niece and nephew?"

"They're not old enough to be a problem yet."

As Seija and Enis talked Katharina and Levi recorded them on their recorder. The two children kept quiet as they overheard what they were saying. As Enis went to leave, they ran away to their rooms.

They played the recorder back.

"What should we do with it?" Rina asked Levi.

"Give it to Dad," Levi suggested.

"No, he would kick out Auntie Seija."

"That would be a good thing."

"But..."

"But nothing."

"Then who do we give it to?"

"How about Ljerka and Taiki?"

"Okay. So, where are they?"

"In the living room with Uncle Marcos."

They ran to the living room. They brought the recorder with them. They stood in the doorway.

"I think we should leave, Ljerka," Taiki said. "Before something worse happens."

"We'll be fine," Ljerka said then looked to the doorway when she heard a yeep. "Who's there?"

Levi and Katharina walked towards them.

"What's wrong?" Ljerka and Taiki asked.

"Nothing..." Katharina started to say, putting the recorder behind her back.

"What do you have?" Ljerka asked. "Give it to me," she ordered.

Levi took the recorder and handed it to Ljerka. "We recorded something we overheard."

"What did you overhear?" Taiki asked.

"We overheard Aunt Seija and Enis talking," Rina answered.

"What did they say?" Marcos asked.

"You should just listen," Levi suggested then played the tape.

As they all listened, Naheem, Kamal, and Tristan walked in. They stood in shock as they heard their sister devious plans with Enis. Once the tape was done, Naheem took the recorder from Taiki and stormed off. Tristan and Kamal stormed out after him.

"Seija!!! Seija!!!" Naheem called at the top of his lungs.

Seija ran towards them as she said, "I'm here! I'm here!" Stopping in front of her brothers. "What wrong?"

Naheem just the played the recorder. As it played, Seija showed no remorse, no shame, no anything but a smirk.

"So, you know," Seija said.

"Yes, we do," Kamal confirmed.

"So, who told you?" Seija demanded. "Was it those two bitches?"

"No, your niece and nephew, Seija," Tristan answered.

"Hm. The two brats," the woman sneered. "They should have died with their mother."

Naheem just struck her in the face.

"Heem, that was..." Tristan started to say.

"Yes, it was, TL," Kamal countered.

"Hm," Seija sneered dabbing at her bloody lip.

"You and your husband are to leave this house," Naheem ordered. "You have two hours to pack your things." then he stormed off.

"So be it," Kamal said then he, also, walked off.

"Where am I going to live?" Seija demanded.

"Should have thought of that before you did what you did and what you said," Tristan said. "Don't bother running to Mom and Dad, either."

Seija started grinning. "I could called them."

"No! Don't even think about it. Leave them out of it."

"No!" she said running off as she took out her cellphone.

"Shit!" he cursed.

"Mom, Kamal, Naheem, and Tristan are being mean to me." Seija wined.

"Seija dear, what did they do?" her mom asked.

"He told me... Juliano and I has to leave."

"What did you?"

"Nothing. Absolutely nothing."

"Ahh, I can't believe they did that."

"I really didn't do anything."

"Okay. So, what you want me to do about it?"

"We need a place to stay."

"Honey, you can't stay with us."

"Why not?"

"We're leasing it to the Dasell's."

"Who are they?"

"A friend of the family."

"Oh, then where are we going to stay?"

"I don't know but, you'll find somewhere."

"Ugh!" Seija huffed then hung up.

Seija then dialed her Dad's number. "Dad?"

"Princess, what's wrong?" her dad asked.

"Naheem kicked Juliano and I out."

"Ohhh, why?"

"I didn't do anything."

"The nerve. You can come stay with me."

"Oh thank you, Daddy!"

"You're welcome, Princess."

Seija talked to him a few minutes later before hanging up. She was grinning as she packed.

Chapter 17

Ljerka, Naheem, Tristan, Marcos, Kamal, and Taiki had a meeting regarding Seija. Ljerka was both angry and shock. Later that night, Ljerka and Naheem lay in bed together. They didn't touch but was close to.

"Naheem?" Ljerka said.

"Yeah?" Naheem said.

"I'm sorry about your sister," she apologized.

"Me, too," he, also, apologized. "I can't believe she said those things."

Ljerka stayed quiet.

"To say those things about her own niece and nephew..." Naheem said.

Before he could finish, the phone rang.

"Hello?" Naheem answered.

"How could you do that to your sister?" his father demanded. "For woman no doubt. She never did anything to..."

"Dad, why are you calling so late?"

"Seija called me saying: you kicked her out for no reason."

"Dad, she..."

"You know she has no where else to go."

"But..."

"You fix it and fix it now."

"Dad, will you listen to me?"

"No, fix it." then his father hung up.

"Damnit!" Naheem threw his phone after hanging it up.

"What was that all about?" Ljerka asked.

"Seija lied to get her way with my father," he explained.

"Oh wow," she said shocked "Seriously?"

"Yes."

"Damn."

"Yeah."

In Taiki's room at Naheem's, Taiki and Kamal lay in the bed.

"Dad must have called Heem," Kamal commented after hearing a crash sound.

"How do you know that?" Taiki wondered.

"Dad rubs Heem the wrong way. Also, Seija is Dad's favorite."

"Being as she's the only girl."

"Correct."

"Damn."

"We can find out what happened tomorrow. No use asking now. Heem is too angry."

"Good idea." snuggling up next to Kamal.

Taiki wiggled her ass on his cock.

"I wouldn't do that if I were you," he warned growing hard.

"Why?" she asked playfully doing it again.

Kamal pushed Taiki onto her back then entered her.

"Aahh," she moans. "No fair. I was just playing."

"Me too," he moaned as he pumping into her.

Kamal set a slow pace as he kissed her.

Ljerka moved to snuggle with Naheem but he wasn't there. She got up and put her night gown on. She then left the room in search of Naheem. She found him in his office drinking a glass of whiskey.

"Naheem?" she called softly.

Naheem looked up. "You should be sleep," he slurs.

"So should you," she countered. "What are you doing down here?"

"Just thinking and drinking."

"Thinking about what?" asked concerned.

"Everything."

"Why?"

"You ask too many questions," he snapped.

"Sorry." turning to leave.

Naheem got moved fast and caught her arm. "Don't leave me."

Ljerka turning towards him as he released her arm to pull into a hung. She just stood there at first before hugging him back.

"I'm sorry I snapped at you," Naheem apologized.

"It's okay," she accepted. "I understand family and favorites."

"I thought you would," he said. "Dad always favored Seija to Tristan, Kamal, and I because she was the only girl."

"And even now, it's happening."

"Yes, it is."

"Nothing you could do now is sleep. Come to bed."

"No, you go on up."

"Not without you."

They stood at a stand still, not moving. They just moved to the couch in the office that was also a pull out bed. They then lay on the bed kissing and touching one another. Naheem disrobed Ljerka as he kissed down her body. He sucked on her clit as he fingered her.

"Aahh...Mm...Aahh," she moans a loud.

She climaxes under his mouth. She feels him enter her wet pussy. "Aahh," She moans again.

"Fuck!" he moans. "You feel so good," as he pumps in and out of her slowly.

Ljerka bites her bottom lip, gently, making him move faster. She moves to meet him. "Aahh," she continues to moan.

"Shit," he moans.

They climaxed together. Naheem empties himself into her then snuggled up to her. They fall asleep.

The next day, Seijia and Enis plot to do something against Ljerka and Taiki again.

"What do you think we should do?" Enis asked.

"I don't know," Seija said. "I'm not living with them no more."

"What?! When that happened?"

"Today, Naheem kicked me out and he know what going on."

"How did he find out?"

"I let it slip and he hit me."

"Oh wow. So, who are you staying with?"

"My dad. He's so gullible."

"Oh."

"Yeah."

Juliano overheard their conversation and got mad. He storms off as he pulls out his phone.

"What do you want, Juliano?" Naheem demanded on the third ring.

"I think they're going to try to do something worse," Juliano informed him.

"They who?"

"Enis and Seija."

"What are they trying to do?"

"I don't know but, they're going to plan something. So look out."

"Thanks, Juls."

"No problem."

The two men hung up.

"Who was that?" Ljerka asked.

"Juliano," Naheem informed her. "Be care seeing your mom and dad today..."

"Okay, I will," she said.

"Matter of fact, I'll take you," he said.

"Naheem..."

"I insist, Ljeri."

"Fine. I'll tell T, you're taking us," walking away.

"Yeah, I'll be upstairs changing." walking with her. "Meet you in ten."

"Okay."

In the car, Ljerka felt like a little child with Naheem driving them to her mom's house. They were silent the whole way there. Once they got to the Haggerty's house, Ljerka kissed Naheem goodbye.

"Call me when it's time to leave," Naheem ordered.

"Okay, see you soon," Ljerka said backing away from the car.

Ljerka and Taiki sat with Dovie in their living room.

"Did Naheem just drop you off?" Dovie asked.

"Yes," Ljerka answered. "My car is in the shop."

"Why?" the older woman asked.

The younger women was reluctant to tell the older woman. "Well..."

"Well, what?"

"We don't want to upset you, Mom," Ljerka said.

"Aw, you called Mom."

"Is that okay?"

"Yes, it is. You're trying to distract me. Why don't you want to distract me?"

"It is upsetting to even say what happened to us," Taiki informed her.

"Tell me anyway," Dovie ordered.

"Okay it's like this: My brakes in my car were cut."

"Marty!" Dovie called for her husband.

"What?" Marty asked.

"Come here," she said.

Marty entered the living room. "Yeah?"

"Listen to this. Say it again, girls," his wife ordered.

"My brakes were cut…" Ljerka informed them.

"Do they know who did it?" Marty asked.

"Yes, Seija did it to try and get rid of us," Taiki answered.

"Seija?" Dovie said shocked. "She couldn't even hurt a fly."

"It seems like she was planning this for year from what I heard."

"How did you hear that?" Dovie then asked.

"The children recorded her and Enis talking," Ljerka said. "There is something else…"

"What?" Marty asked.

"Seija and Enis may have, also, killed Eve," Ljerka informed her parents.

"What?! They did what?!" Marty voice boomed as Dovie cried.

"I'm sorry," Ljerka apologized. "Dad? Mom?"

"What are you sorry for?" Dovie demanded. "You did do anything wrong."

"I'm still sorry, Mom."

"Okay. Thank you for tell us," Marty thanked her.

"We finally know who this to her," Dovie said.

Chapter 18

Ljerka and Taiki went back to Naheem's home where Tristan, Marcos, and Kamal waited. Naheem pulled into the driveway and parked the car. The women look solemn, almost sad. The guys did everything to cheer them up but, it didn't work.

"What's wrong, honey?" Marcos asked.

"We told Mom and Dad, what could possible have happened to Eve," Ljerka informed them.

"You told them, what happened to Eve?!" Naheem demanded. "You had no right…"

"I had every right, Naheem," she said.

"You weren't family until four or five months ago," he exclaimed.

"I see how you feel now."

"Damnit!" Naheem cursed. "That's not what I meant."

"Yes, you did," Ljerka accused then stormed off.

"I didn't mean it!" he yelled down the hall.

"You better fixed that," Taiki ordered. "I need to live with her at the end of the day, you don't," then stormed off.

"Shit, bro, you made enemies of the only two women linked to Eve," Kamal said.

"Shit!" then Naheem stormed off in search of Ljerka.

When Naheem found Ljerka, she was packing. He stood blocking the doorway as he knocked on the doorway panel.

"So, you're doing to leave," Naheem stated.

Ljerka didn't say anything.

"You're not going to talk either," he then stated. He walked over to her to pause her hands.

She snatched her hands away and began to pack again.

He grabs the suitcase and puts it to the floor. Before she could grab it, he pull her into his arms.

She slaps him in the face then struggle in his arms. "Let me go, Naheem!"

"So, she can talk but can she listen?" Naheem said.

She slammed at him again. Only this time, he caught it before her hand connected then kissed the top of it.

"Hm," she said trying to pull her hand away.

As he continued to kiss her hand, Naheem took each one of her fingers, one at a time, into his mouth and sucked gently. "I'm sorry," he apologized. "but when it comes to family problems, I like to keep in the family."

"I thought the Haggerty's were apart of your family," she moaned.

"They are but they are in- laws."

"Eve was their daughter. I'm their daughter..."

Dropping his hand and arm away from her before he talked. "You didn't know until you got her four or maybe five months ago."

Walking out his arms as she said. "Yea, I know. If someone didn't email me about this place, it would never have..."

"I know. Meeting you has been like... seeing you been with you, made me feel like I was with Eve again."

"I'm not Eve."

"I know. I knew that since you got here but,..."

"But..."

"I've come to love you as Ljera and not as Eve."

"You love me?"

"Yes, I do. Almost from the first time I've met you," walking toward her.

Once Naheem was in front of Ljerka, he framed her face and kissed her. He wrapped his arms around her as he did so.

"Do you still was to go?" Naheem asked.

"Yes..." Ljerka answered.

"But..." he said.

"I have to get back to work. Taiki maybe my boss but..." she said.

"I understand. What if you moved her with the children and I?"

"I can't, Naheem. You know I can't."

"Shit, Ljerka."

"I know. I know."

"Do you, Ljerka? Do you?"

"Naheem..."

"You could see your parents all the time if you lived here."

"That's not fair."

"I know but I had to try to get you to stay."

"Yeah."

Meanwhile in the living room, Taiki and Kamal were having the same conversation. She had to leave and they could stay forever. Their vacation time was coming to an end soon. This was the last week they were going to be in Goldenleaf.

"I could come with you," Kamal said.

"No you can't. You need to stay here and help Naheem and Tristan help Seija and Enis in check," Taiki countered.

"True but I thought you were going to stay until Tristan and Marcos' wedding and to see their new twins."

"We are but after that we are leaving." getting up to distance herself from him.

Getting up and wrapping his arms around her. "I'll come visit when I'm free that is."

"You better," she said turning in his arms.

They kiss then move apart.

Later that night, Ljerka, Naheem, Taiki, and Kamal went to Tristan and Marcos' wedding rehearsal. Marcos' family was introduce to Taiki and Ljerka. The Decartes was shocked to find out the Haggerty's had another daughter. One that looked so much like Eve.

As it became later, Marcos and Tristan asked Taiki and Ljerka to be the best women in their wedding. Since Marcos didn't have any friends to be his best men. They accepted the request to stand up with them.

"Thank you, Ljerka. Taiki,"Marcos thanked them as he hugging them both.

"You're welcome," Ljerka said hugging him back.

"Any time," Taiki said hugging him back.

"Are you two going to have bachelor party?" Ljerka wondered.

"Yes, a joint one," Marcos said. "You two are invited."

"Oh, thank you," Taiki said.

"Can't wait. When?" Ljerka said excited.

"Tomorrow night," Tristan said.

"We'll be there." Ljerka said.

Tomorrow night at Tristan and Marcos' Joint Bachelor Party, everything decorated in colors of blue and silver. Tristan wore silver where as Marcos wore blue. They sat the head table in the middle of the yard with their friends and family at tables around them.

Everyone was having a good time until Tristan's parents began drinking. They were making a scene. Miranda and Angelo Lukas were drinking hard as they always did.

"Mom, you and Dad need to leave," Tristan said. "You two aren't going to ruin my Bachelor Party."

"I'm not leaving. It's everyday my gay son gets married," Angelo slurred.

"Right, TL, we're happy for you," Miranda slurred.

Kamal got up to help his brother. "Come on," he said ushered his parents out. "I'll drive you home."

"No!" Miranda and Angelo yelled.

"Don't wait to go," Angelo slurred liked a little child.

"Well, you're going," Naheem said firmly as he join them.

Kamal ad Naheem ushered their parents out the party. The brothers piled them into a taxi that someone, at the party, called. They told the taxi driver their address then sent them on their way.

Kamal and Naheem went back to the party and saw everyone crowded around Tristan and Marcos comforting them.

"Everything okay?" Naheem asked rubbing Tristan's back.

"Yeah, now it is," Tristan reassured him.

"Baby, you know you are not okay," Marcos said.

"Marcos, I'm not letting that bother me," Tristan said.

"Good. Not until after the wedding," Marcos said. "We'll deal with it then."

"Right," Tristan then kiss Marcos' lips.

They kiss then family and friends cheered. It wasn't even the wedding kiss.

Chapter 19

After the wedding the next day, the wedding reception was coming to a close. It was almost time for Ljerka and Taiki to leave. They gave them their best wishes. Kamal and Taiki and Naheem and Ljerka drove back to Underfield Spring House. The women grabbed their suitcases and bags. They got into Taiki's car and loaded up the car. They said their goodbyes. They drive off.

Something started malfunctioning in Taiki's car. The steering wheel started to not work.

"Something is wrong," Taiki said.

"What's wrong?" Ljerka asked worried.

"Something wrong with the steering wheel."

"Oh damn!"

Taiki realized then the brakes weren't working. Taiki tried the emergency brake and that didn't work, also.

"Call Naheem or Kamal!" Taiki ordered.

"Okay," Ljerka said pulled out her phone. "Naheem, the brakes and the steering wheel doesn't work," she said into the phone.

"Aahhh," the women screamed as they flew a red light.

"What's wrong?" Naheem demanded.

"Just come help us!" Ljerka screamed.

"Where are you?" he asked.

"Just outside Eastbourne Falls heading to…" she said.

"Aahh!!!" the women screamed.

Naheem hears Ljerka's phone go dead. He calls Kamal to let him know what going on.

"Where are they now?" Kamal demanded.

"I don't know. Ljerka's phone cut off before she told me," Naheem explained.

"I'm on my way," his older brother said then hung up.

The brothers drove to where they think Ljerka and Taiki were. They saw ambulances and fire fighters at the scene. They stopped when they saw Taiki's car all banged up. They got out the car and ran over to it. They were stopped by two police officers.

"We know the women in that car!" Naheem yelled as he fought against the officer.

"You can't go over there," the officer said.

"Just tell me they are okay," he said.

"We're not at liberty to tell you that," another officer said.

"Damn it!" Naheem cursed before punching the officer in the face knocking him out.

As Naheem was getting arrested for assault, Kamal ran over to the car to see no one inside. He heard Taiki calling his name. She was at one of the ambulances holding an ice pack to her head.

He ran over and kissed her passionately. "I was so scared," he said.

"I'm alright but Ljerka is pretty banged up," Taiki said worried.

"How banged up?"

"She unconscious. She... she..."

"It's alright. It's alright."

"They're rushing her to the hospital once, she has someone to go with her. Where is Naheem?"

"Getting arrested."

"Not funny, Kamal."

"I'm not joking. Look."

Taiki looked over a the officer's car Naheem was in back of. "Shit!"

"Yeah," Kamal agreed.

"What did he do?" she wondered.

"Punch the officer for not letting us through," he answered.

"Wow."

Ljerka lay in the hospital bed with tube up her nose and in her arms. Naheem walked in the room and sat in a chair next to the bed. She was started to come to when he took her hand. She turns her head towards him.

"Naheem?" Ljerka called with a raspy voice.

Naheem's eyes shoots up to Ljerka's face. "You're awake," he said with a relieved smile. "How are you feeling?"

"In pain and thirsty," she said. "Where am I?"

"In the hospital," giving a sip to drink.

"Hm, ouch."

"I'll get the nurse."

Naheem got up and walked to the nurses' station. "Ljerka Tarrant is up." then the nurse and doctor followed him the room.

"Hello, how are we leaving?" the Doctor asked.

"I'm in pain," Ljerka answered.

"I'll give you something for the pain after I look you over. Could you step out a minute, sir?"

"Yes, I'll be outside." walking out into the hallway.

As he waited, his phone rang.

"Hello?" he answered.

"So, how is she?" Kamal asked

"She just woke up. The doctor is in with her now."

"Oh thank god."

"Yes. How is Taiki?"

"She has a headache but she's fine."

"Oh okay."

The doctors decided to keep Ljerka another night.

The next day, Ljerka went home. Naheem drove them to Ljerka and Taiki's apartment. Once they were outside, he carried her up the stairs to her room.

"Heem, will you put me down?" she requested. "I'm fine."

"No, you're not," he countered walking to her bed then laid heron it. "You were…"

"I know what I was but I'm fine now."

"Hmp," was all he said.

Taiki came into the room as they were arguing. "I see you are feeling better."

"I am but Naheem, here, won't leave me alone," Ljerka said annoyed.

"I will once…" Naheem stated fluffing up her pillows.

"Will you stop it? Leave us alone a minute, will you?"

"Fine." he gave in leaving.

"Why are you treating him like that?" Taiki asked sitting on her friend's bed.

"Heem is being annoying," said Ljerka.

"He thought he lost you. He punched…"

"He punched someone…"

"Yeah, a police officer."

"Oh my…"

"Yeah, he thought he lost you. I thought the same thing."

"Aw, I'm a fighter. I'm never going to leave you alone."

They hug as Kamal and Naheem walks in.

"Look at this, bro," Naheem said.

"I see it," Kamal said. "What brought this on?"

"Nothing," Ljerka and Taiki said in unison, letting each go.

"You two are not tell the truth," Naheem said.

"For real, it's nothing, Heem," Ljerka assured him then she fake yawns. "I'm tired I'm going to bed." getting comfortable.

"We better go," Taiki getting up to leave. She pulled Naheem and Kamal with her. "She needs sleep."

They left Ljerka's room and went into the living room. Taiki went to bed, also, leaving Kamal and Naheem to bunk out in the living room.

"Seija and Enis are being dealt with at home by Jaxon and Maxim," Kamal informed his brother.

"Good and call the police to arrest them," Naheem said.

"Are you sure you want to get our sister arrested?"

"Yes, they had the women in my life and the woman in yours killed."

"She's blood."

"She should have thought of that before," Naheem said before going for bed.

Kamal sighed and followed and suit.

Epilogue

Two months later, Naheem, Ljerka, Taiki, and Kamal were in Goldenleaf. Taiki and Ljerka had moved there three weeks before. As they settled in, Taiki moved in with Kamal at Underfield Autumn House. It was the mirror of Underfield Spring House.

Later that night, Ljerka and Naheem lay in bed.

"Are you happy?" Naheem asked.

"Blissfully," Ljerka relied.

"I want to ask you to marry me and be a mother to Katharina and Levi. Maybe give me more children."

"What's stopping you?"

"After everything that happened, I thought you might not want to."

"I want to marry you. All you have to do is ask me."

"Ljerka Tarrant... I mean Haggerty, will you marry me?"

"Yes." then kissed him passionately.

Don't miss out!

Visit the website below and you can sign up to receive emails whenever Cheyenne Scrivens publishes a new book. There's no charge and no obligation.

https://books2read.com/r/B-A-HEZT-MWBZB

BOOKS2READ

Connecting independent readers to independent writers.